ROUND MOUNTAIN

ALSO BY CASTLE FREEMAN, JR.

All That I Have
Go With Me
A Stitch in Time: Townshend, Vermont, 1753–2003 (history)
My Life and Adventures
Judgment Hill
Spring Snow: The Seasons of New England (essays)
The Bride of Ambrose and Other Stories

Round Mountain

TWELVE STORIES BY

CASTLE FREEMAN, JR.

CONCORD
FREE
PRESS

Published by Concord Free Press
152 Commonwealth Ave.
Concord, Massachusetts 01742
www.concordfreepress.com

Designed by Alphabetica
www.alphabeticadesign.com

Round Mountain was printed by Kodak. Cover printed on a **Kodak NexPress** Digital Production Color Press with **Kodak NexPress** Dimensional Clear Dry Ink. Book block printed on a **Kodak Prosper** Press on 50# Uncoated Freesheet - Warm White paper, converted on a **Hunkeler** Book Finishing Solution, and bound on a **Bolero** Perfect Binder. Kodak, NexPress and Prosper are trademarks of Kodak.

ISBN: 978-0-9847078-2-9

This Book Is Free.

By taking a copy, you agree to give away money to a Hurricane Irene relief organization or a charity of your choice. When you're done, pass this book on to someone else (for free, of course), so they can give. It adds up.

Round Mountain is a special project of the Concord Free Press, Kodak, and Vermont author Castle Freeman, Jr. And you're part of it. For more information—and to tell us where you gave—go to WWW.CONCORDFREEPRESS.COM/ROUNDMOUNTAIN

This Book is Fr[illegible]

[illegible]

INTRODUCTION

On Round Mountain

by Pinckney Benedict

When I was a boy, I used to have the privilege, though it seemed natural enough to me, of spending much of my time alone. I grew up on my family's dairy farm in southern West Virginia, and my mother felt perfectly comfortable sending me out on those long-ago mornings with a lunch pail in my hand, a little pump-action Marlin .22 over my shoulder, and perhaps fifteen long-rifle cartridges, for plinking, in my pocket. I developed a powerful taste for solitude and forested places in those days, even though the woods of our farm were (I see now that I am older) thoroughly domesticated.

Later, I sought out wilder fastnesses farther from home. I recall with almost painful nostalgia the way that, in certain places high in the Alleghenies, the woods—the trunks of the trees so close, their canopies so lush, the undergrowth so dense, that you could feel sometimes that you were not outside at all, but rather that you were standing in a small intensely green windowless room of deep secrets and almost unbearable beauty—would suddenly open up to astonishing and unsuspected vistas: plummeting waterfalls, wild rivers veined with rapids, and vast fossil-marked sandstone monoliths hulking together like the buildings of some forgotten Paleolithic city.

Round Mountain is a book like that, exactly like those panoramic outlooks hidden in the woods of my boyhood. How small (comfortingly at first, and then distressingly) this world of lovingly-drawn rural people seems, on first encounter! And how vast it is revealed to be, when we push forward towards its end: impossibly vast, terrifying and gorgeous, as dangerous and as intoxicating as any mountain wilderness.

How luxuriant is the accretion of character details across these dozen stories! And how polished the stories are, without ever being cold. How quiet without ever (not for a moment) turning dull. How dry, how droll, without any sacrifice of seriousness. How tragic, without ever indulging in maudlin or manipulative emotion. How visionary: the climax of the title story—a story that puts its writer in the legendary company of folks like Welty and O'Connor—enters unabashedly into the realm of prophecy. The world of *Round Mountain* seems, on first blush, quite small; but it is in truth vast and glorious, filled with fear and awe.

It is a world that, once you have entered it, you will not want to leave, and that you will never forget.

Carbondale, Illinois
May, 2011

Table of Contents

1 Driving Around

9 The Gift of Loneliness

21 The Poor Brothers

45 The Women at Holiday's

63 The Montreal Express

71 Bandit Poker

85 An Incident of the Late Campaign

103 Say Something?

119 The Sister's Tale

127 Charity Suffers Long

147 Round Mountain

169 The Deer at the End of the Day

Driving Around

TWO KIDS, A BOY AND A GIRL, high schoolers playing truant, were riding in the back of Clay's Wagoneer. Homer and Clay had picked them up in the village. They were going to near Dead River.

"You know Carmichaels'?" the boy asked. He was talking to Homer.

"Sure," said Homer.

"Past there."

"The trailer?" Homer asked him.

"Back of the trailer," said the boy.

The kids had been in front of the store when the men stopped for coffee. Homer and Clay were driving, just driving around. They had been halfway to Brattleboro to see a man who was supposed to have a used compressor for sale. The man wasn't home, and they had come back over the mountain. At that time, Clay was still strong, but his eyesight was affected, and his attention was liable to stray. He couldn't do much, but he could drive around. That is, he could be driven around.

He and Homer enjoyed each other. Their outings gave Clay's wife a break. And, then, he got the fresh air that way, the conversation. He got the stimulus. Say what you like, it's better than TV—well, maybe not a lot better.

The two kids didn't have much to say. Those kids never do. They rode in the back, holding hands. The girl held her boyfriend's hand in her lap. They both looked a little shot, as though they'd been up all night. They sat silent in the back. They weren't much for company. The boy might have said ten words the whole time. The girl didn't say one.

May Day: they passed yellow daffodils spotted here and there, singly or in clumps, over the pale, winter-beaten land like little flags stuck in the ruins of a defeated city. May Day: season of renewal; youthful season of obscure rural passion. By no means a restful time of the year. The cruelest month, plus one.

"What's that on your arm?" Clay had turned in the passenger's seat to address the kids in the back. He wanted to engage them. He was talking to the boy. "Is that a tattoo?" he asked him.

The boy was wearing a gray T-shirt, and the muscle of his skinny upper right arm was encircled by a tattooed bracelet, black or dark blue in color.

"Is that a tattoo?"

"I guess," the boy said.

"You guess?" said Clay. "It looks like barbed wire. Is it supposed to be barbed wire?"

"I guess," the boy said.

"Well, what's it for?" Clay asked him. He smiled, nodded at the boy. "You know, what's it mean?"

In the rearview mirror, Homer's eyes also watched the boy.

"I don't know," the boy said. "Nothing."

"Ah," said Clay. He turned back to face forward. He shook his head. "Some kind of tribesman, you think?" he said to Homer. Homer grinned.

Ahead of them the road ceased to be paved. The Wagoneer came down hard onto the dirt, then bounced along.

"They're working at that place up behind me," Clay said to Homer presently. "That camp."

"Holiday's," said Homer. "It ain't a camp."

"Not Holiday. Some other name. Morgenstern, Mortonson? Some name like that."

"That's right," said Homer. "It was Holiday's. His place. We still call it Holiday's. It ain't a camp."

"I remember Holiday."

"No, you don't," said Homer.

"Well, they're working up there, this past week," Clay went on. "They've got something running up there, banging away all day long, some machinery."

"Well driller," said Homer. "Rusty's putting in a well for them. That's Rusty's rig you hear. I understand he's gone down five hundred feet and got nothing. That's all ledge, up there, too. It must run a couple of hundred dollars a foot."

"I hope Morgenstern's rich, then," said Clay.

"So does Rusty," said Homer.

•••••

Driving, just driving around. Driving around is something you have to count on doing a certain amount of in those parts, but how you do it—how you sort it out—depends on your age, and it depends on your sex.

Driving around has its modes and structures. You get your license when you turn sixteen. Then boys drive around with boys, exclusively, girls exclusively with girls. By and by, boys begin to drive around with girls, girls with boys. The boys do the driving. Then, say in your mid-twenties and thirties, boys drive around with boys again, and girls don't drive around at all. That's because earlier, when boys and girls were driving around together, they weren't driving the whole time, and so there are little kids at home requiring their mothers' care. Through middle age, you find boys driving around with boys once more, and girls driving around with girls. And finally, going into the golden years—the season of rest, the last of life, for which the first was made—the boys and girls are together again, though now it's mostly the girls who do the driving, owing to the boys' being so old, crippled, blind, and crazy that they're a menace on the highways—rather like Clay, except Clay hadn't quite reached the golden years as yet, nor was he going to, it didn't look like.

"How does your wife like it?" Homer asked Clay.

"Like what?"

"You know, the well driller running all day long next door."

"Not much. You know what she said?" Clay asked him. "You know how it pounds away—*ga-whump, ga-whump, ga-whump*—you can feel it as much as hear it. She said it sounds like three a.m. at Motel 6."

"She said that?" Homer asked.

"She did."

Homer laughed. "She's right, you know it?" he said. "Up and down, in and out, pumping right along, shaking the walls—it's like a dirty movie, ain't it?"

"How do you know about those movies, a country boy like you?" Clay asked him

"Somebody must have told me," Homer said.

"Around the bend up here," the boy said from the back.

Homer brought the Wagoneer into a driveway on the right. There was a trailer with a little porch or stoop made of two-by-fours and fifty feet behind it a log cabin building, new. Both were apparently empty, with nobody home, no vehicles to be seen, only an old dog who came slowly out from under the trailer's porch when they drove in.

"Here you go," said Homer.

"Thanks," said the boy. The girl opened her door and got ready to leave the car.

"By God," said Clay, "She's got one, too." The girl looked around.

The boy was following her. "What?" he said.

"A tattoo," said Clay. When the girl got out of the Wagoneer, they could see on her right ankle a blue circlet on the skin, like her boyfriend's.

"Some kind of Hottentots," Clay said. The girl giggled.

The boy shut the door, and the two of them started toward the trailer.

"Say hi to your father," Homer called after them. The boy turned.

"I will," he said. He followed the girl around the trailer toward the house in the rear. Passing beside the trailer, he stopped to pat the dog, but the girl went on ahead.

Homer backed out of the driveway and got them headed on toward the hamlet of Dead River Settlement. Presently the pavement resumed and they went smoothly.

"You know those kids?" Clay asked Homer.

"Don't know the girl," Homer said. "The boy's Andy McAuliffe's kid. Brendan. He's a ballplayer. He'll be graduating next month."

"A ballplayer. Pitcher? Outfielder?"

"Basketball."

"An athlete," Clay said. "A tattooed athlete. It's a new world, isn't it? Do they do that to show they're going together?"

"I wouldn't know," said Homer.

"My day, you gave her your class ring," said Clay. "That way, if it didn't go well, she'd give it back to you. What are these kids supposed to do, in that case?"

"Maybe they ain't worried about it not going well," Homer said. "Looks like it's going pretty well so far, don't it? Cut school, go back to your girl's place, spend the afternoon, just the two of you, her parents ain't home. It could go worse."

"You mean you didn't do that when you were in school?" Clay asked him. "I did. Did it all the time."

"Sure, you did," said Homer.

"I imagine they'll be doing their homework, don't you suppose." Clay went on. "Their Latin, their conic sections, history. Of course, it isn't all work. They'll play with the dog—nice looking dog. Maybe a couple of games of checkers, game of gin, watch a little TV."

"Now you're showing your age," Homer said. "Checkers? Gin? TV? You've got to get caught up a little, here, you know it? They're going to be getting on the computer, is what they're going to be doing. Getting on the Internet."

"Getting on something, anyway. The Internet? That's how you know about those movies, isn't it?"

"Me?" Homer said.

Dead River Settlement was seven houses. Three stood on the hillside above the road, four below the road down the bank toward the river. One of the lower houses had burned the winter before. The fire had started in the chimney and burned out the attic and the roof, leaving the rest of the house intact but uninhabitable. You could look down from the road, through the blackened rafters, into the rooms on the upper floor. You could see the old-fashioned flowered wallpaper, the water pipes, the bathtub, the doors, the broken windows, their filthy, ragged curtains. In one of the rooms the bed had been left, a stripped brass rack. The yard in front of the burned house, and the ground to either side of it, were littered with burned clapboards, burned shingles from the roof, scorched insulation, tarpaper, and scattered bricks from the fallen chimney; but there, too, yellow daffodils stood in clusters, blooming and nodding in the air above the wreckage.

A backhoe was parked in front of the house. They were excavating the foundation. The building had been jacked up off its cellar and supported by timber cribs. Sometime in the days to come, a crew would run rails under the house, shift it onto a flatbed, and haul it away.

Today, waiting for them, the house stood open above and below: its gaping roof and dark cellar both full of light and air. The building seemed to hover between the earth and the sky, like a house in a child's drawing.

"I thought they'd have taken it by now," Clay said.

"This week," Homer said.

"Where is it going?"

"Connecticut someplace."

"Connecticut? I thought just down the hill. All that way on the back of a truck?"

"Why not?"

"Well, I'd think they'd take the frame apart, move it, then put it back up. That's how I'd do it."

"Fellow bought it don't want to do that," Homer said. "Chestnut frame. Belongs in a museum. He'd rather pay to truck it. I heard he gave Billy Wingate a hundred and fifty thousand just for the frame."

"A hundred and fifty thousand? The place is worth more after it burned than before."

"About ten times more," said Homer. "Billy was tickled. He said he wished he'd burned the place down twenty years ago, but he missed the cat."

"That kind of money," said Clay, "this whole state will be on a truck to Connecticut."

They rode out of Dead River, over the bridge, and beside the long pasture of the Perkins place. Ed Chauncey had his truck in the pasture with a load of posts and wire. During the winter a car had left the road in a snowstorm and hit the fence, knocking a section of it over. Ed was there to put it back up. He worked for Perkins. Homer waved to him as they passed, but Ed had his back to the road.

"Now, for tattoos," Homer said. "I see it this way. I don't mind the young guy's. I don't mind a guy having a tattoo. Maybe he's been in the navy."

"Maybe he's been in jail," said Clay.

"Maybe he has. It's his business. But that little girl. What's she want with a tattoo?"

"You said it was to show she and the guy were going together," Clay said.

"You said it, not me. I don't know. I don't know what a girl wants with a tattoo. Does she think it's sexy?"

Perkins had cows. He'd let them out, fifteen or twenty of them, and they stood about in the pasture, singly, not grazing, not doing anything, staring, as though they'd forgotten why they were there.

"Monica's got one," Clay said.

"A tattoo? She does?"

"She does. A little, tiny rose, about as big as your thumbnail."

"Is that right?"

"That's right. You wouldn't have seen it, though."

"Oh. How did she happen to get a tattoo?"

"I don't know. It was before I knew her. She won't tell me."

"Maybe she'll tell me. I'll ask her, one of these days."

"No, you won't," said Clay.

No, Homer wouldn't ask her. Were he to, Monica would know he and Clay had been talking about her as they were driving around. She would know they talked about her as they talked about so many things, passing things, unimportant things, amusing things: the two kids, the well driller, the burned house, Perkins's cows. Monica might have thought she was one of those things. She wasn't. Her tattoo, its origin, its location, wouldn't come up, not in this life. But as they left the pasture on their right and entered the woods, Homer thought of that little, tiny, pretty, hidden rose.

The Gift of Loneliness

THE LITTLE OFFICE AT RAYMOND'S, behind the bays, was always hot. Alva had rigged a fifty-five-gallon drum in there as a stove. It burned a drip of dirty motor oil. It was a good stove, but you couldn't turn it down. Clay took off his coat. He hung it behind the door on one of Alva's pegs. Homer hadn't arrived yet. The room was too hot, too small, and it had no window. Still, the three of them met every afternoon for coffee at Raymond's. There was not a lot to do, and you had to do it someplace.

Clay turned to ask Alva about Homer, but Alva's helper, out in the bays, began running the compressor.

"Can't hear you," said Alva.

"Where's Homer?"

"Not here," Alva said. He was making the coffee. The compressor stopped. "Coming now," Alva said.

They heard Homer come into the garage and stop to talk with Alva's helper. Homer came into the office. While he was taking off his coat, Alva's radio commenced to squawk from its shelf above the coffee machine.

Tone Pasture Mountain fire, Pasture Mountain, please. Respond to Spring Road, District Two, for a tree down in the road...uh...wires also down, and hot. Wires are hot. Meet the power truck. Pasture Mountain, please. Spring Road.

Homer hung his coat behind the door next to Clay's. Alva had the Rutland paper on the desk. Clay took out his glasses and put them on to read it, but it was two days old.

"You got today's?" he asked Alva.

"Billy's got it out there," said Alva. "You can get it from him, if you don't mind its all-over grease."

"I don't know why you can't get two papers," Homer said. "One for him, one for in here. It seems like the least you could do, us coming in here every day to keep you company."

"You mean if I started not getting any paper you'd leave me alone?" Alva asked.

"He didn't say that," said Clay.

The radio gave a long chatter, then began again.

Tone is for Rockingham rescue: respond to Goose Mill Road, Mount Pleasant. Doolittle residence. Eighty-eight-year-old male subject on the floor. He's okay but he can't get up...uh...they've got a dog there. Rockingham, please, Rockingham: Goose Mill Road, Doolittle. Subject down. Look out for the dog.

"If I get so old I can't get up off the floor by myself, you can shoot me," said Alva.

"You're that old now," said Homer. Alva grinned. He shook his head. He poured out their coffee.

"What's he doing down on the floor in the first place?" Clay asked. "Why did he get down there if he can't get up?"

"Probably he dropped his teeth," said Alva.

"Probably he dropped a nickel," said Homer.

"Probably he was looking for truffles," said Clay.

"What's truffles?" Alva asked. He put the three cups on the desk.

Each of them fixed his coffee: Homer with sugar and milk powder, Alva with sugar only, Clay with nothing; he took his black. Alva sat in the desk chair. Homer sat in an old canvas chair to Alva's left. Clay leaned against the steel filing cabinet in the corner. He drank his coffee standing up. There was no chair for him.

"It don't make it any easier for them, does it?" Alva said. "Do you remember that thing at Taft's?" he asked Homer.

"When?"

"Oh, years ago," said Alva. "Twenty-five, thirty years. That dog he had?"

"I heard about it," said Homer.

"Heard about it?" Alva said. "You were there."

"No."

"Who's Taft?" Clay asked.

"Inborn Taft," Alva said. "Lived way out on the way to Back Diamond—not even in town, if you want to be technical. Years ago. Called the rescue, said he was having a heart attack, I don't know. Chest pains. Terrible, he said. So we all got the ambulance, went on out. You were there."

"No," said Homer.

"Inborn?" Clay asked.

"That was the man's name," said Alva. "Ask him."

"That was his name," said Homer.

"So, we all get out there with the ambulance," Alva said. "Valentine's driving the ambulance. And we pile off and go tearing up to the house, and *whoa*. There's this dog out front. Huge thing. Police dog. About as big as a calf. And just wild: snarling and snapping and lunging around—got to get past him to get into the house, you see, start Inborn's heart back up for him. You were too there."

"I was away," said Homer.

"Away, where?" asked Alva.

"What happened?" Clay asked Alva.

"Yeah," said Alva. "Well, so everybody's standing around looking at Inborn's dog, there. And finally Valentine's got like a loudspeaker in the ambulance, like a bullhorn, you see. And he goes gets it and stands in front of the house and gets on the bullhorn, and he says, *You want us to do you any good in there, you get out here and call off your fucking dog.*"

Alva laughed. "*Call off your fucking dog!*"

"So?" Clay asked him.

"So, what?" said Alva.

"So, did he?" asked Clay.

"Sure," said Alva. "Inborn comes out, moaning and groaning, grabbing his chest, grabbing his side, going, *Oh, God, Oh, God.* Kicks the dog into the house. We go on ahead, examine Inborn, go over him, get him situated."

"Heart attack?" Clay asked.

"Course not," said Alva. "Probably he was drunk."

"He generally was," said Homer.

"Where were you, then?" Alva asked Homer. "I was sure you were along that time. Where were you?"

Alva's radio interrupted them:

Tone is for Dead River rescue: respond to MVA, Porcupine Road. Lady went into the brook...uh...not in the brook...over the bank. Dead River, respond to Porcupine Road about two miles past Cavanaugh's. MVA... uh...They need a wrecker.

Alva put his cup on the desk and got to his feet. He took his coat from its peg behind the door and the keys to the wrecker from their hook beside it. Alva kept the wrecker keys on a ring he had wired onto a metal pie plate, painted red, so they wouldn't be easily mislaid.

"Do you want company?" Homer asked him.

"No," said Alva. "I won't be long, it don't sound like. That coffee's gone when I get back, it ain't going to be pretty."

"We'll watch it for you," said Clay.

Alva went out through the bays. They heard the wrecker start up, and then they heard its back-up beeper as Alva brought it around into the road. They heard the wrecker drive away.

"I hope that's not Leila or one of her girls," said Clay. "That's their road."

"I doubt it is," Homer said. "It will be somebody from away, I expect, some tourist."

Clay smiled. "What makes you think so?" he asked.

Homer shook his head. "What?" he said.

"How do you know it's nobody you know?"

Homer looked puzzled. He shook his head again. "I don't know," he said.

Clay took up the coffee pot and filled Homer's cup and his own. Then he sat in Alva's chair. Outside in the bays Alva's helper began banging on something with a hammer. He was hitting hard on something solid: a string of ten or a dozen heavy, regular blows. *Bank... bank...bank...bank.* Then he quit.

Clay tasted his coffee. "I saw Angela," he said. "Friday, Thursday. One day last week."

"That's more than I saw her last week," Homer said.

"She said Quentin—" Clay began, but Alva's radio opened up again.

Tone Valley Fire. Valley, please: respond to Blackway residence, Schoolhouse Road, Post Factory. Smoke in the house. Valley for smoke in the house, Schoolhouse Road. Blackway.

"I don't see how he stands having that thing on all the time," Clay said. "It drives you nuts."

"The scanner?" Homer said. "You got to have a scanner. Everybody needs a scanner. How else do you know what's going on?"

"There's such a thing as knowing too much of what's going on, son."

"I won't argue that with you," said Homer. "But you got to have a scanner. A scanner's better than a nosy neighbor. You don't have a scanner?"

Clay smiled. "You know I don't," he said. "Do you?"

"You know I do. Got a couple of them. One for the truck."

"Come to that, I guess you've got the nosy neighbors, too, don't you?"

"Them, too," said Homer.

"Angela said Quentin's starting school next year."

"No," said Homer.

Raymond's was as neat, as well-ordered, as the cabin of a little vessel. You might have packed the whole place up and shipped it to the Smithsonian. In the office, in the bays, Alva kept the tools, the supplies, the benches, the workspaces picked up and sorted out, and he kept the whole place swept. You have seen garages that looked as though they had been hit by a hurricane followed by a mudslide. Raymond's was not that kind of garage. Alva had thought of everything, had a system for everything, and made sure his helpers knew the system and kept it. In the office, you saw Alva's way in the coat pegs behind the door, in the coffee machine, in the radio on its shelf above the coffee machine, in the pie pan key ring for the wrecker. In the bays you saw it in the rows of black fanbelts of different sizes that hung like bats from nails driven into the rafters overhead, three belts on each nail; you saw it in the good light, the clean, dry floor, the mechanics' high tool chests that rolled around on casters, even in the sign Alva kept above the office door, the famous garageman's sign:

LABOR
$20 per Hour
With You Watching: $30
With You Helping: $50

Alva's life outside Raymond's was evidently of a piece with the rest of it. He lived in Dead River Settlement in a house where he kept ducks and bees. He kept his wife there, as well; they had been married forty years. They had two sons, both grown, both nearby. One was in the Post Office, one was in the State Police.

"She said he's starting first grade," Clay said.

"No," said Homer. "He's not starting anything."

Homer. What about Homer? Looking at Homer, you would have said he was Alva-in-training, Alva's younger brother or cousin. You'd have been right, too: in fact they were cousins, though remotely. But you'd have been wrong. Homer looked like Alva, but he wasn't like him. For all his measure and repose, Homer's life in those days was like a ball of snakes that he pulled around behind him in a child's wagon wherever he went. Homer's wife, fifteen or twenty years younger than he, had moved out and was living with her current boyfriend in the next town. She and Homer hardly met, hardly spoke. Their son lived sometimes with her, sometimes with Homer, mostly with Homer's sister. He didn't know where he lived. There was something wrong with him. He hadn't been able to go to school. Maybe now he could. The wife and the sister thought so.

"No," said Homer. "It's just she's got some doctor who's been working with him. I don't know, some kind of specialist. Thinks he's got a vitamin deficiency. Can you beat it? All these years. Just get him topped up for vitamins, he'll be fine. Well, Angie believes it, Cal believes it."

"But you don't," said Clay.

"No."

"Why not? Maybe it's true."

"Maybe it is," said Homer.

Tone Dead River rescue. Dead River. Cancel MVA on Porcupine Road. Sheriff's there, wrecker's there. No injuries. Lady's okay...uh...little bump on the head is all. Refused treatment. Dead River, go on home.

"They're already there," said Homer.

"Sure, they are," said Clay.

"Better make fresh," said Homer. He left his chair and went to the coffee machine. He took the old coffee grounds in their basket and dumped them in the pail under the desk.

"You don't know, though," said Clay. "You can't tell. Everybody's on his own schedule. Look at Einstein. Wasn't it Einstein? Somebody like that. He could hardly tie his shoes 'til he was ten or twelve. Took forever to learn to read. Everybody thought he was a moron. He wasn't. He was Einstein. He was on his own schedule."

"This ain't Einstein, here," said Homer. He poured water into the coffee machine and switched it on.

"How do you know?" Clay asked him. "You don't know. That's the point. I knew a kid, myself," he went on. "When I was in school, there was a boy in my year who everybody thought was the same way, slow. More than slow. He never talked, had no friends, wasn't on any of the teams. Never changed his clothes, never cut his hair. Never knew his lessons, failed in every class. He was hopeless."

"How come they kept him in the school, then?" Homer asked. "If he failed everything?"

Clay smiled. "Well, his father was some kind of Rockefeller. At that school, if your father was a Rockefeller, you didn't have to be a real good student. If your father was a Rockefeller, you were okay with them."

"This one's father ain't a Rockefeller," said Homer.

"No," said Clay. "But with this kid I'm talking about, he came around. What I'm getting at is, he turned out fine. Know what he's doing today?"

"No."

"He's governor of Colorado."

"This one ain't going to be governor of Colorado," said Homer.

"Maybe not," said Clay. "The point is, he's on his own schedule. The point is, he'll get where he's going."

"The point is," said Homer, "he's not going anywhere."

Tone for Ascutney rescue. Respond to Windsor Middle School. Thirteen-year-old female subject...uh...locked herself in the girls' bathroom, second floor...uh...says she's got a weapon...says she'll injure herself. Ascutney rescue, respond to Windsor Middle School. Respond to the principal's office.

Middle school. What is that, seventh grade? Sixth? It don't make it easier. Easier? It's impossible. A thing like that is impossible. Why call the rescue? Call her parents. Maybe they did. Maybe it was her parents who called the rescue. They had to call somebody. What will happen? Nothing good: degrees of bad. You'll probably never know. The trouble with the radio is, you hear the beginning of the story, but you never hear the end.

Homer sat down in Alva's desk chair. The coffee was made. They watched it run into the glass pot. The machine turned itself off. Alva would be back shortly.

"Where's the doctor he's going to?" Clay asked Homer.

"White River."

"What is he, a pediatrician?"

"She," said Homer. "It's a woman doctor. I guess she's a pediatrician.

I don't know."

"In White River?" Clay said. "Look, take him to Boston. There's all kinds of doctors there."

"We took him to Boston."

"New York, then."

Homer smiled. "They got better people in New York than in Boston?" he asked.

"Always," said Clay.

Outside the office Alva's helper started up the compressor again: five long bursts. *Brraap, brraap, brraap, brraap, brraap.* He must have been working on somebody's wheel with the lug wrench.

"Can't hear you," Clay said.

"I said about New York. You're a New Yorker."

"Once upon a time."

"What part of town?"

"Central Park West," said Clay.

"When I was a kid," said Homer, "I lived in New York. Not for long. Farther up. Way uptown. Near the college up there."

"Fordham?"

"The other one."

"Columbia."

"That was the one," Homer said. "I went down there one winter. I was just out of school, eighteen. Never been in a city. Never seen a tall building. I had a room in a kind of hotel. They called it a hotel. Seven bucks a week. Amsterdam Avenue."

"Amsterdam Avenue," said Clay. "You a New Yorker. I wouldn't have thought."

"I wasn't one long," said Homer. "I was down there, I guess, five or six months."

"What did you do?" Clay asked him.

"What did I do? I worked. I had to eat."

"Worked doing what?"

"Oh," Homer said, "about anything. I washed dishes. I was a messenger boy. I ran an elevator; they gave you a little suit to wear."

"Sure, they did," said Clay. "Elevator operators. You're talking about the Middle Ages, here."

"Amsterdam Avenue was Irish," Homer said, "but the Spanish were moving in. From Puerto Rico. The Irish hated them, but it looked like that wasn't going to make a lot of difference. The Irish kept to themselves. They didn't say much. The Puerto Ricans made more noise, all night, every night. I don't think they ever went to sleep."

"The Middle Ages," said Clay. "Amsterdam Avenue? The Irish are long gone. The Puerto Ricans, too, I guess."

"Who's there now?" Homer asked him.

"I can't tell you."

"I didn't see anybody down there like me," said Homer.

"You mean from here?"

"No," said Homer. "I mean like me."

"You didn't know anybody," Clay said. "Nobody knew you. If you live there, you're supposed to like that. That's the gift of loneliness, son."

"Yes," said Homer. "But I thought it was funny, you know? All those people, millions. More people in a couple of blocks than in this whole state. Nobody."

"So you came home." "I came home," said Homer. "Not because of that. My big brother broke his leg. June. Just at haying. He couldn't help Dad. Dad couldn't do it alone. I came home."

"That's where you were the time Alva was talking about," said Clay. "When they had the call on Back Diamond with the fellow who had the dog, the fellow with the name."

"Inborn," said Homer. "Inborn Taft. God, Inborn must be dead ten or fifteen years, too, by now."

They heard the back-up beeper sounding outside as Alva, returned, brought the wrecker into its place beside the building. They heard one of the wrecker's cab doors slam, then the other. They heard Alva speak to his helper outside in the bays. Then the door to the office opened, and a woman came in. Homer had been right about her: she was nobody any of them knew. Above her left eye she had a blue bruise that was beginning to come up.

Alva came in behind her. He hung the keys to the wrecker on their hook beside the door, then turned to look at the woman.

"You took a pretty good shot, there," said Alva. "You're going to have a goose egg. I wished you'd let them take you to the clinic."

"A goose egg?" the woman said.

"A lump," said Clay. "A swelling where you cracked your head."

"Oh," said the woman. "No, really. I'm fine."

"Well, then, here you go," said Alva. "You can call your party from here if you want. Or one of these guys can probably take you where you're going. They ain't good for much, but either one of them can drive a car. You want coffee? It ain't very good coffee."

"I can't take her," said Homer. "I'm going to work."

"I'll take her," said Clay.

"Coffee would be lovely," said the woman.

The Poor Brothers

From around the bend behind, car lights sprang up and fixed Homer like a deer. He got off the blacktop and walked in the rough grass at the side of the road. The lights grew, filled the night, slowed, and then a big car came up behind Homer on his left, two feet from his hip, its color white, a car like a courtesan's bed: Junior's rolling pleasure dome.

The rear passenger's side window rolled down. Homer bent. His friends were there, in the car's dark recess lit only by the useless glimmer of the dash: Junior and the Captain—but not alone. Somewhere they had picked up a girl, her perfume or cologne mingled with the smell of beer that came to Homer from the car's interior. They had found a girl. Who would she be? There were no girls.

"Kind of close, there?" Homer said. He looked into the car. Not one girl, he saw, but girls fore and aft, one in back with the Captain, in the dark where Homer couldn't see her. The other girl, the cute one, was up front with Junior.

"I said, you came kind of close, I thought," Homer said.

The girl in front laughed in the window and turned to Junior. Junior, offspring of a bear and a fox, educated by a billy goat, by trade a summer housepainter and a winter navigator on warm, azure seas. He leaned across the girl's body toward the window, his right arm around the girl's mostly bare shoulders, his left hand holding a can of beer on the glowing dashboard. Junior thrust his face into the window.

"I missed you, didn't I?" he asked Homer. "I missed you. We're bullfighting here, Homer. The closer I come the better it is, long's I miss. Jump in. It's Homer, Cap."

"Can't be," the Captain said. "Homer's gone."

"He doesn't look gone to me," Junior said. "He look gone to you, baby?" he asked the girl beside him.

"No," she said. "He looks thirsty." A blonde girl wearing jeans and something on top that stopped short and showed her middle.

"Give him a beer, then, baby," Junior said. The girl reached down to the floor of the car and brought up a can which she tossed out the window. Homer caught it.

"I don't mind," Homer said.

"Sure, great," Junior said. "Jump in. Night's young. Get the door for him, Cap." He turned to the girl beside him and tried to kiss her, but she turned her face, laughing, and pushed him back behind the wheel. "You're the *driver*, baby," she said to Junior.

"You know I am, bunny," Junior said. He put the big white car in gear.

The Captain opened the rear door for Homer. Homer got in beside him and shut the door. Junior made the car's tires kick the gravel beside the road. They were under way.

"That's right, too," Junior said. "You're not supposed to be here, are you? I thought you'd be gone."

"Next week," Homer said.

"Where's he going?" the girl in front asked.

"Leaving Cheyenne," Junior said. "Going west. Going to follow the sun. Going to make his fortune."

"Ha," the girl in the back seat said.

Was that funny? Homer looked over toward her, but she was in the corner and he couldn't much see her with the Captain between them. He drank his beer.

"Going to follow the sun," Junior said. "Right, Homer?" He hit the car's horn, which had a sound in four notes: *bee BEE, bee BOO.*

The blonde girl laughed at that. "Check out the car," she said.

"Coupe de Ville," Junior said. "Fifty-four. Practically an antique."

He struck the steering wheel with his fist. "One of the goddamndest most foolish cars ever built. Weighs most of two tons. Detroit iron, none of your Japanese chickenshit. Runs like a top."

"You must work on it a lot," the girl said.

"Pussy cat, I *do* work on it a lot. I work on it *all* the time," Junior said. "I work on it, and I work on it. I am an expert, baby. Isn't that right, Cap?"

"Absolutely," the Captain said. Older than the boys, and by a good deal. Mild, indulgent, remote—or maybe just drunk. Captain for no reason. Captain of nothing.

"My brother had an old car like this," the girl in front said. "He did a lot of work on it. He had to send away for parts and everything."

"Not me," Junior said. "I got all my own parts. All original. All good. Real good. You'll see. Isn't that right, Homer?"

Homer smiled and shook his head. He finished his beer and dropped the can to the floor where it clanked amongst a dozen empties.

He said, "Got another one?"

"Attaboy, Homer," Junior said. "Get down." He hit the horn again: *bee BEE, bee BOO.* They went left where the road divided in the woods and started up a long hill. On the left, the steep side of Round Mountain and across the road a drop of twenty feet to the boulder fall where the brook ran down the mountain to join the river in the intervale.

"Where are we going, man?" the girl in the back seat with Homer and the Captain asked.

"Lady wants to know where we're going, Cap," Junior said.

"She knows," the Captain said.

"Going up to the monastery, right, Cap?" Junior said. "Going up to visit the monks."

"The poor brothers," the Captain said.

"Well," the girl asked, "they got a ladies' there?"

"A ladies'?" Junior said. "You mean a bathroom? With plumbing and a door and like that? Sugar, you're up in vacationland now. Up here a ladies' is low-growing thistles. Come *on*. A ladies', for Christ's sake. Hear that, Homer?"

"We could stop at Curry's," Homer said.

"You want to stop at Curry's, Cap?" Junior asked.

"Why not?" the Captain said.

"Okay, but I don't like it," said Junior. "What happened to pulling over and pissing in the weeds? This country's getting soft, too."

"I'm floating," the girl said.

They had come to Dead River Settlement, seven buildings along the road: six houses, the old Dead River Grange, and Curry's, on past the last house. Junior stopped short of the gas pumps. Both the young women got out. They walked together into the light above the pumps.

Junior, the Captain, and Homer watched them. Now Homer saw that the girl from the rear seat who had said *Ha* was black. A black girl, tall, and wearing some kind of white or maybe silver dress that was cut short and made her legs look longer than Sunday afternoon. Her friend was a head shorter, a soft yellow blonde, and between the halter that covered her chest and stomach and the jeans that covered her bottom there were visible six inches of beach-brown skin.

Junior looked after them. He leaned forward and rested his chin on the steering wheel.

"Boys," he said. "We have got us a sundae. What do I say? I say, thank you. Thank you, Jesus."

The girls went into Curry's. The bell over Curry's door jangled.

"Who are they?" Homer asked.

"Hookers," Junior said. "They've got to be. Hookers on holiday: the country boy's dream come true."

"What makes you think they're hookers?" Homer asked.

"Jesus, Homer, look at them," Junior said. "Look at their clothes. Look how they move. They look like the Evening Star to you? Besides, they gave us wrong names. What did they say their names were, Cap?"

"Daisy Buchanan and Becky Sharp," the Captain said.

"Daisy is the nigger," Junior said.

"Well," Homer said, "so those are their names. What about it?"

"What about it, Cap?" Junior asked.

"Those aren't their names," the Captain said. "Those are book names."

"They were on the bus from New York," Junior said. "With Cap. They all tumbled off together. They've been pissed all day. Cap's pissed too, aren't you, Cap?"

"There and back and getting there again," the Captain said.

"We were going to stock the camp," Junior said. "Everything's in back. We're going to take them on up there out in the woods and show them what hospitality really means. You can learn a lot from those girls, Homer. Even the Captain, old as he is, is willing to learn. What do you say? They'll give you a hell of a send-off."

"I don't mind," Homer said. "I'll need another beer, though."

"We'll all have one," Junior said. "Go on in and pick up a case."

Homer started to get out of the car, but the Captain held him back in his seat.

"My party," the Captain said. He opened the door of the car on his left. "My party," the Captain said again.

"Way to go, Cap," Junior said.

The Captain was in worse shape than he seemed. When he got out of the car he nearly fell on his face beside Curry's gas pumps, but he found his feet and made his way to the store, where he took hold of the door handle and held Curry's tinkling door open for the two girls, who were just then coming back out.

"Guy's shitfaced," said Junior, watching him from the car.

"What was he doing on the bus?" Homer asked.

"Who knows?" Junior said. "What was he doing in New York? Who knows? When did he go there? Who knows? Not him. Shitfaced. At least he came home with some action."

The girls returned to the car and got in, and the two of them and Junior and Homer waited for the Captain to come back with the beer.

"God, it's so quiet," the blonde girl, Becky Sharp, said. "There isn't a sound."

"What do you mean?" Junior said. "Hear that? Fall's coming."

The night air that came in the car windows was thronged with the ringing of crickets.

"That's not a sound," said Becky.

"Well, then, listen to my heart," Junior said, and he gently pulled her head onto his chest, but Becky sat back up, giggling, and pushed him away.

"But that's not a sound, either," she said.

"But that's not my heart, either," said Junior. Becky ruffled his hair with her hand, laughed at him, and kissed him slowly on the mouth.

"*Mmmm,*" said Junior.

"How was that, baby?" Becky asked him.

"That was pretty good," Junior said. Becky put her hand on his belly and kissed him again. When they parted, Junior turned to Homer.

"He ought to been out by now," Junior said. "Go on in and see what's keeping him."

Homer got out of the car and went into Curry's. When he walked into the heat and light of the store, he thought he was beginning to be a little drunk, too. Curry was at the counter beside the door. He had just rung out the Captain's case of beer. He looked at Homer like a cop.

"He's in the back," Curry said.

Homer went to the rear of the store, where the toilet was cramped in behind the coolers. He opened the door and went into the toilet. It was full of the smell of disinfectant and the heavy, fake cherry smell of the soap Curry put in the urinal. Homer thought he could smell the faint perfume of one of the girls, too. The toilet was the cleanest place in the store.

The Captain was in there. He was standing at the sink, leaning on it, and looking at himself in the mirror that hung above it on the wall.

"That fellow doesn't like me," the Captain said.

"Who?" Homer asked him.

"That fellow out front."

"Curry?"

"He thinks I'm a bum," the Captain said. "He thinks I'm drunk."

"Well," Homer said.

"He's not far wrong," the Captain said. "I am drunk, but he is not even that."

"Are you ready?" Homer asked him.

"Has he got our beer up?"

"It's there,"

"Then I'm ready," the Captain said.

"Listen," Homer said. "Do you want to just go on back home? Tell Junior. Tell him to take you home."

"Lord, no," the Captain said. "No point in going there. Besides, what about the, ah, ladies?"

"What about them?" Homer said. "Junior and the one are about in bed already. Let him take them. Junior can take them both."

"I doubt that," the Captain said. "I doubt that very much. Let's go."

When he stood up from the sink he nearly went over backward, so Homer got him around the waist and walked him out of the toilet and toward the front of the store. When they reached the door the Captain was walking by himself, but he walked as though he were six or seven feet above the ground. The bells above the door jangled.

"Get him out of here," Curry said to Homer. Homer picked up the case of beer from the counter in front of Curry and went out after the Captain.

•••••

Two miles past Curry's they left the blacktop and turned right onto a dirt road that went over a concrete bridge and into the woods on the other side of the brook, here only a couple of feet across. Now and then the woods opened, and they passed a barn or a house, sometimes with a light showing, sometimes dark, and then the woods came down to the road again, the leaves on the August hardwood trees passing dusty and pale in their headlights. They continued to climb up the mountain, and by the time they had driven ten minutes from the blacktop the houses had stopped, and the places they passed where the woods parted were not cleared land but bogs, reed-grown and full of killed trees, their sharp bare trunks standing in black water.

"Do you know where you're going, man?" the black girl, Daisy, asked.

"To the monastery," Junior said from the front. "Tell her about the monastery, Cap."

"The poor brothers," the Captain said.

"That's them," Junior said. "The poor, humble delvers in the wasteland. What kind do you call them? Sounds like sisters?"

"Monks?" asked the blonde girl, Becky. "You mean monks, like nuns?"

"Cistercians," the Captain said.

"That's it," Junior said. "They can't live in towns or near other people. They only live way out in the woods. Like bears."

"Oh, yeah?" said Becky. "How many monks?"

"Let's see," said Junior. "How many brothers are in residence at this time, Cap, do you know offhand?"

"At this time?" the Captain said.

"Yes, at the present time," Junior said.

"Three, at present, I believe," the Captain said.

"There's three of them, baby," Junior said.

"How did I guess?" said Becky Sharp.

•••••

Junior brought the car off the dirt road where a pair of wheel tracks went into the woods. He drove in the tracks for fifty feet among the trees, the car tossing like a boat at sea, the trunks and branches leaping in the headlights. Junior stopped, turned off the engine.

"Okay," he said.

Homer got out of the car and closed the door. The Captain and the girl Daisy got out, then Junior and Becky. The trees were thick about them, and the young women looked uneasily around and then up, where overhead, through the black, tangled branches, a couple of stars were visible in the sky, like birds trapped under a net. Off to the right something made a crashing and thumping in the woods.

"God, what's that?" Becky said.

"It's a deer," Junior said. "A deer spooked. Nothing to worry you, sugar lump. Your Junior knows these woods like any Indian."

"God, what a place," Becky said. "What do we do now?"

"A little stroll, through the forest," Junior said. "Half an hour, no more."

"To the monastery, right?" Becky asked.

"That's right, angelfood," said Junior. "To the poor brothers. Will they be glad to see you! Got some things to carry in."

Junior went to the rear of the car and opened the trunk. He gave Becky a pile of blankets to carry and took out a flashlight which he gave to her to hold.

"Shine it in here, that's it, baby," Junior said.

"What's this stuff?" Becky asked.

Junior found a paper bag in the trunk and loaded it with a bottle of kerosene, matches, a pound of sugar, a can of coffee, a carton of cigarettes.

"For the brothers," Junior said.

The Captain had sat back down on the rear seat of the car and stretched out along the seat on his back.

"How are you doing, Cap?" Junior asked.

"Feel lousy," the Captain said. "I think I'll stay here."

"Come on, Cap," Junior said. "Don't crap out on us, here. What'll the poor brothers say, you don't come to lead them in prayer?"

"Lead them, yourself," the Captain said.

"I can't, Cap," Junior said. "You know I can't. I'm not ordained right. Come on."

The Captain groaned.

"Cap?" Junior said.

"Alright, alright," the Captain said. "I wouldn't want to let the brothers down."

He rose wearily from the seat.

"Course not," Junior said. He turned to Daisy. "Do you think you could kind of hang onto Cap, there, a little, moonbeam?" he asked her.

"Kind of get him pointed right? He's a little under the weather. That's good. Homer?"

Junior reached to the front of the trunk and dragged out a heavy cardboard box. "Can you get this?" Junior asked Homer. "I'll get the rest. Come on, sugar lump."

Homer leaned into the trunk and picked up the box. It clinked. On the top was printed in red:

JOHN JAMESON & SONS: DUBLIN: IMPORTED.

"That's for the brothers, too, right?" asked Becky.

"They use it for cleaning," Junior said.

Becky and Junior, with the light, led the way along a narrow path that was cut through the woods. Behind them the Captain and Daisy walked side by side. Daisy put out her hand to steady the Captain when he took a false step and looked like going over. Homer took the case of whiskey under his arm, settled it on his hip, and followed them. With every step he took, the bottles rang gently together in the box, a pleasant sound like the call of a little night bird.

They were going in to the Captain's deer camp. Homer had never been there, but he had been in places like it. Several of the men in town had camps up in the high woods among the mountains to the west of the village. You'd have a shack, ten by fifteen or a little better, made of boards and tarpaper or pole logs; tin roof, or more tarpaper. Inside a couple of canvas bunks, a table, chairs maybe and maybe no chairs, and an oil-drum stove with the rusty pipe going out the wall. The place would be on a knoll in the woods near a brook or beaver pond for water, as far from the road as you were willing to carry whatever materials and equipment you thought you needed. You'd go there twice a year: once in the late summer or early fall to see where the deer were and to bring supplies that the damp and the porcupines would destroy if the stuff were left in the camp, and once again in November for hunting. The Captain's place was supposed to be the best one in town: it had been part of a logging camp years before. It was bigger than most. It was also the most isolated camp, sitting beside a long pond in a dip under the highest ridge of Round Mountain.

Junior walked beside Becky. The path was easy to follow. Becky pointed the flashlight around and above, playing it over the cave of trees they walked through. Carrying the bag of groceries in one arm, Junior had slipped his other hand into the rear pocket of Becky's jeans, and they walked together, with his hand on her bottom and the light swaying above them like an enormous bat.

"These monks really live remote," Becky said. "I'm glad I'm not a monk."

Junior patted her bottom.

"Me, too," he said. "Me, too, baby."

Behind them, Daisy had let the Captain go ahead of her. She took up beside Homer.

"How are you doing?" Homer asked her.

"I'm allright," Daisy said. "I don't know if the older guy's going to get there, though."

"He'll make it," Homer said. "It's his place."

"How much farther?" Daisy asked him.

"I don't know for sure," Homer said. "It can't be much."

"You don't know?" Daisy said. "You been there, man?"

"No," Homer said.

"No?" Daisy said. "But you're with them, right?"

"Sure," said Homer.

"Uh-huh," said Daisy. "You're Homer, right?"

"That's right," Homer said.

"Homer," Daisy said. "Where are we going, for real, Homer?"

"Deer camp," Homer said. "The Captain's camp. A cabin, kind of, off in the woods. For deer hunting."

"Hunting camp, huh?" Daisy said. "I've been to hunting camps before, man. I never saw a lot of hunting done at one, though, except guys hunting me. It's a party house, right? When we get there, we party?"

"That's right," Homer said.

"My girlfriend will like that," Daisy said. "She'll go anywhere on a party. She was once on a party on a guy's plane that went around the world—you know, flew around the world, partying the whole time. Went on a week."

"Were you there, too?" Homer asked her.

"Me? No, man," said Daisy. "Does that sound like a black folks' party to you?"

"I don't know," Homer said.

"You don't know," Daisy said. "Well, I'm telling you."

Ahead of them the Captain was in trouble. He had walked into a small tree. He stepped back, and sat down heavily. Daisy left Homer and went to him. She helped him up and they went on. Homer waited. He saw that Junior and Becky had reached the camp. It was a long, low building. Beyond it the woods opened, and Homer could see starlight and a surface of still water, and in the far distance, a wooded ridgeline black against the sky. Junior opened the door of the camp. When Homer came up, he had the flashlight inside and was looking for the lamps. The Captain was inside the camp with Junior. Homer set the case of whiskey down on the ground. He and the two young women waited outside for Junior to get a light.

•••••

The Captain's camp was a building that had been one of the bunkhouses of the lumber company's gang that had cut the timber from Round Mountain around the time of the First World War. The loggers' other buildings—the cookhouse and office, the stables, the tool sheds—had long since fallen into the ground, but the sleeping quarters had been kept up. It was made of big pine logs, peeled, and it was shaped like a ship: thirty feet long and no more than ten feet wide, with a low ceiling. The door was in the narrow end of the building, bunks along the walls, then benches and a big table. In the opposite end wall somebody had built a stone fireplace, and somebody had built windows into the two long walls.

"This is it?" Daisy asked.

"Sure is," Junior said. "Old logger's place. Nice, huh?" He was getting the lamps ready.

"I thought you said it was a hunting camp, Homer, man," Daisy said.

"It is," Junior said.

"God," Becky said. "You mean you guys live in here?"

"Sometimes," Junior said.

He had the lamps going, five or six of them, and the end of the long room was lit with the dark, unhelpful light that kerosene gives.

Junior had opened the case of whiskey and was getting glasses off a shelf beside the fireplace. Homer sat on the table in front of the fireplace, and the two young women stood on either side of the mantel. The Captain sat in a busted rocking chair beside the cold fireplace and looked from one to another of them as though he had never seen them before. He had taken a hard hit from the tree.

"I'm waiting to see the monks," Becky Sharp said. "Wonder where they're at."

"Where are the poor brothers, Cap?" Junior said.

"What?" the Captain said.

"The brothers, Cap," Junior said. "The Cistercians. Where do you suppose they've got to?"

"Vespers," said the Captain. "They may be gone for some time."

"What goes on here, then?" Becky asked. "What do you do here?"

"Deer camp," Junior said. "Pursuit of the elusive whitetail. Think about it, baby."

"Hunting camp, right," Becky said. "My brother went hunting with my dad. All they did was get drunk and play cards. It's a joke."

"It's no joke," Junior said. "Here's to it."

He had filled five glasses with pale golden whiskey, and he handed them around.

"Irish whiskey," Becky said. "A guy I know drinks this. You've got like a couple of hundred dollars worth of booze here."

"It's Cap's," Junior said. "He drinks it like water, don't you, Cap?"

"I don't drink water," the Captain said.

"Long life," Junior said. They drank.

"What do you think, Homer?" Junior asked.

The fumes of Homer's first swallow of the Captain's whiskey had risen from this throat into his nose and made his eyes water. He blinked.

"I don't mind," he said.

"*Jaysus*, look at the little bugger suck it in," Junior said. "And me the only real Irishman in the room. Or am I? I don't think you'll be Irish, now, are you, acushla," he said to Daisy.

Daisy laughed. "Black Irish, man," she said.

Junior went to Becky then, put his arm around her bare waist and his face in her hair. "What about you, peaches?" he said. "I'll bet you're as Irish as Paddy's pig. Speak to me."

Becky laughed and leaned in against Junior.

"German Jewish," she said.

"Saints and angels!" said Junior. "A daughter of Abraham. Becky Sharp, is it?"

"Yeah, well, we changed it," Becky said.

Homer drank his whiskey. He shut his eyes, opened them. He looked at the others. Each of them, he saw, was surrounded now by a kind of finer light like a halo, a brighter light that crowned their bodies, shimmering. The Captain, Daisy, even the bottle on the mantelpiece, each stood in glory, and a single crown of light surrounded the united figures of Becky and Junior. Homer blinked. He shook his head.

The room smelled of hot lamp oil, old air, mice, and faintly of tar. Homer set his glass down on the table he was sitting on. He tried to get off the table, he put one foot on the floor.

"Where are you going?" Junior asked.

Homer stood in front of the table. He turned and started for the door of the cabin. He bumped into a chair. Homer swung his arm and knocked the chair across the room.

"Look out, Homer, Jesus," Junior said.

Homer stood before the door. He had hold of it, but it wouldn't open. He pushed at the door. It was fast.

"Are you going to puke, Homer?" Junior called from the other end of the room.

Homer kicked the door. It held fast. He kicked it harder, cracked the board.

"Pull it, Homer, for God's sake," Junior said.

"That young fellow wants out," the Captain said.

"These country boys, you know?" Junior said. "They take on a little too much and before you know it they're kicking down the walls."

Homer was outside. He stood before the camp for a few minutes until he could see a little in the dark. He shut the door behind him. Then he went down to the pond. Nothing moved out there, no fish jumped, and the night was ruled by the big flank of the mountain, possibly the summit, possibly not, that slanted against the sky at the end of the water, blocking out the stars.

Homer walked beside the pond until he saw, not far from the camp, a little point that stuck out into the water with a big pine tree growing on it. He went to the tree. Somebody had sawed off the lower branches for fifteen feet above the ground and had nailed wooden cleats or steps ladderwise up the trunk to a platform of boards fixed to the heavy branches above. You could take your gun up there and wait for the deer to come to the water or to the opening near the camp. The deer wouldn't look for you overhead. Homer had waited with his father in stands like that one from the time he'd been seven or eight. His father had been a keen hunter. Homer had seen him kill a running deer with one shot at two hundred yards, the length of the river piece at Johnson's. They walked over the rows of chopped stalks together, and when they came to the dead deer his father got down on one knee.

"You'll never see another shot like that if you live to be a hundred and five," his father said. "Not if you stay around here, you won't." It was true. In their country of woods and brush and corners, you learned to shoot not long but quickly, and so his father had been right. But Homer hadn't cared much for hunting, and he wasn't going to stay around there. The thing was, Homer was moving away, to a broader country where if you cared to do it you could take shots every season like the one his father had made at Johnson's. A country without trees.

Homer pissed against the pine tree. His water foamed like beer in the needles at the foot. He leaned against the tree on his straight arm. Out there you pissed on what? Grass. *There is too much in me, but I will hold, I will not burst. Instead of bursting I will wait until what is inside me can be let into a different vessel, stronger, more shapely, above all, larger.*

Homer was back at the camp, listening at the closed door. The Captain had shut up. Homer opened the door and stopped. He saw at the other end of the room in the yellow lamplight Junior and Becky, both naked, together on the rocking chair. Junior sat in the chair and Becky was on his lap, straddling him. Junior was bucking her gently and saying, "Okay, all right, okay." The Captain was stretched on the long table near them like the corpse at a wake, evidently passed out. The black girl, Daisy, wasn't in the room at all. While Homer stood in the doorway, looking in at Becky and Junior, Becky jumped off Junior's lap and pushed the chair over backward. Junior landed on his head against the wall, but he got right up and went after Becky, who shrieked and ran around the table. Junior followed her. "Come on, baby, come on, now," he called to Becky, but she skipped lightly around the room ahead of him, holding her breasts in her hands and shrieking happily like a jay. The Captain didn't move.

"You want to grab her, there, Homer?" Junior called. "Make yourself useful, a little bit?"

"Where's the other?" Homer asked. "Where's Daisy?"

"Couldn't say," Junior said. "We've been kind of busy. You want to lend a hand?"

He made another run at Becky, but she darted around the table, keeping it between her and Junior.

"Come on, Homer," Junior said. "Head her."

Homer turned and went back outside and down to the pond. There he found Daisy wading in the shallows. She had her white dress on, but her shoes were on a rock near the water.

"This is all scum in here, man," Daisy said.

"It'll be clean a little way out," Homer said. "They're getting into it back there." From the camp came the bump of falling chairs and Becky's yelps.

"My girlfriend's okay," Daisy said. "He won't do anything she doesn't want him to. She is in charge."

"I guess she is," Homer said.

"So, Homer..." Daisy said.

"Yes?"

"What are you doing, man? What is it going to be?"

"I don't know," Homer said. "What do you think?"

"You know what I am?" Daisy asked. "You know where I'm from?"

"No."

"I was born, Barbados," Daisy said. "You know where that is, man?"

"No."

"The islands," Daisy said. "Caribe. You go there?"

"No," Homer said. "Junior does."

"Junior goes," Daisy said. "Not Homer. Well, you ain't missed much. You ever been anyplace?"

"Here."

"Anyplace else?"

"No," Homer said. "But I'm going."

"Yeah?" Daisy said. "Where to?"

"California."

"California," Daisy said. "That's a long journey, man."

"Yes."

"You going alone?"

"Yes."

"When?" Daisy asked him.

"Next week," Homer said.

Daisy held her dress up around her hips and waded into water to her thighs. She stopped.

"No, man," she said.

"Why not?"

"What are you going to do out there, Homer?" Daisy asked. "For work. Are you going to do my work?"

Homer didn't say anything.

"You know what my work is?"

"I thought I did," Homer said. "The Captain says Daisy's not your real name."

"Why not, man? What's the matter with Daisy? You think Daisy can't be a black girl's name too?"

"I don't know," Homer said.

"The Captain says it. But what is he, that Captain? That Captain is no captain, right? Captain of nothing, him. That Junior? What is he? Paints other people's houses, man. Paints other people's houses and drives around in that ugly car. Those two. I know those two aren't going to no California, man."

"No," Homer said. "Not them. Me. I'm going."

"No chance, man," Daisy said. "Those guys in there are lots older than you. They're lots smarter. What makes you think you're going if they aren't?"

"Next week," Homer said.

"Never going to happen, my child," Daisy said.

Homer was silent.

"See, Homer man, you got it wrong," Daisy told him. "You feel like, well, you got to pour it out into a bigger pot or it will bust, but you don't. The pot won't bust. The pot will work on it and change it. All you got to do is wait. The pot will turn it into some other stuff that won't bust. I'm talking about some kind of stuff that won't even want to bust. Then you're all set, man. For now, though, you got to hang on.

Let the pot do the work."

"How do you know it will?" Homer asked.

"How do I know?" Daisy said. "Come on out here, man. Let's swim. Get your gear off you and come on out here."

Standing now nearly to her waist in the black water, she crossed her arms and pulled her dress over her head. She tossed it up onto the bank at Homer's feet.

"Here I come," Homer said.

He began to take his shirt off. Daisy waited, stood in the shallow water under the tree stand and waited for him. He got the rest of his clothes off and went in after her.

Daisy waited for him in the water waist deep, a half-woman in the dim light, starlight, that came off the pond. Homer reached her. He went up to her. She looked levelly into his eyes. She was a tall girl; they were the same height. Homer put his arms around Daisy, and when he felt her he said, "Oh." But then Daisy threw both her arms straight up over her head, dropped her knees, and slipped like an eel down and out of his arms. He knelt and grabbed for her and held one of her legs for an instant, but she was as slick and strong as a trout, and she dived into deep water and disappeared. Homer reeled backward, flailing and splashing, fell, and went under. He came up again full of water that streamed off him, he coughed and spat the water out and found himself in the shallows. He made his way to the edge of the water and sat down in the mud.

"You there, man?" Daisy's voice came over the water from the direction of the camp.

"I'm here."

"You didn't drown?"

"No."

"You're not much of a swimmer, are you, man?"

"No."

"That's okay, though. Stick to the land, if you can't swim."

"Yes."

"I got to go, now," Daisy said.

"I know."

"Give it time, man. All it takes is time. Just do it like everybody else does. You be fine."

After a while Homer stood. He was cold and shivering, but he was also used up. He felt as if his limbs, his head and neck were full of sand, heavy, lolling. He stumbled about on the bank in the pine needles. He couldn't find his clothes, didn't know where he'd dropped them. Daisy was gone. Her dress was gone, her shoes. The camp was quiet, and although Homer could see the door standing open, the room inside was dark. They had put out the lamps.

Homer walked naked through the trees, away from the camp. The branches caught his skin. When he reached the big pine tree with the ladder steps leading up the trunk he stopped and looked up into the branches where the hunters' platform was fixed. He would go on up there. He climbed the steps with difficulty, and when he reached the platform he sat and leaned his bare back against the trunk. Homer closed his eyes. He lay himself out on the boards.

•••••

The birds waked Homer, the birds, the cold, and the sun. He couldn't keep his eyes closed against the light. Somebody below was calling him.

"Homer, come on, you dead?" It was Junior. He was on the ground beneath the tree stand. Homer leaned over and looked down.

For a moment he didn't understand what he saw. Junior was calling him from the foot of the tree. Junior was naked too. His shoulders, chest, and belly were covered with springy brown hair.

"Let me see you," Junior said.

"What?" Homer said.

"Stand up and let me see you, damn it," Junior said. Homer stood.

"Ah, shit," said Junior. "They got you, too. Sure they did. Bitches. You know where your clothes are?"

"What?" Homer asked.

"Where are your clothes, Homer?" Junior asked.

"They're over there by the water," Homer said. "Aren't they?"

"No, they aren't," Junior said. "They took our clothes, Homer. Clothes, money. My money, what I had. Cap had better than three hundred bucks on him, he figures. They took it. Come on down. I don't look any better from up there."

Homer climbed down the ladder.

"Jesus, what happened to you?" Junior asked him. Homer's chest, arms, belly, and thighs where cut and scratched. "Maybe you made out all right last night, after all," Junior said.

"No," Homer said. "I went through the woods here, got cut up some, I guess."

"I guess," Junior said. He led the way back to the camp. There the Captain waited for them. His skin was pink, and the hair on his chest was mostly gray. His nose and the skin under his left eye had turned the color of an eggplant. When Junior and Homer reached him, he looked them up and down.

"Which one of you is Adam and which is Eve?" the Captain asked.

"How are you doing, Cap?" Junior asked him.

"No worse than I deserve," the Captain said. "Why do we do it?"

"Homer caught up with the chocolate drop," Junior told the Captain.

"Did he?" the Captain said.

"He didn't get it on," Junior said. "He says."

"He says," the Captain said. "He knows better. What did you and that dark girl do out there, boy? What did she tell you?"

"Nothing," Homer said. "We didn't do anything. She didn't tell me anything. I didn't do anything with her."

The Captain was looking at him. "Alright, then," he said. "If you tell me it's so, then it's so. You didn't."

"Neither did I," Junior said. "I don't think I did, anyway. I feel like I'd been dragged over a real shitty road by a long team of horses last night, but I don't feel like I'd got laid. Okay, they did us. They got our money. They got our clothes. They even got the Irish. I don't seem to have my keys, so I expect they got the car. What do we do?"

"Well, we can't stay here like Cro Magnon," the Captain said.

"You'd be allright, that pelt on you; the boy and I'd freeze. I say we draw lots to see which one finds a fig leaf and walks out."

"Draw lots?" Junior said.

"Well, you and the boy draw," the Captain said. "I'd never make it."

"You cut down on the sauce, there, Cap, and you could do it," Junior said.

The Captain looked at him. "Cut down, yourself," he said.

"Cap's embarrassed," Junior said. "What's everybody going to say, he comes dragging into town, bare ass, beat all to shit, cleaned out in his own backyard by a couple of hundred-dollar tarts? Cap's worried about his standing in the community, see?"

The Captain snorted.

"I'll go," Homer said. "I don't mind."

"You're going to walk into town like that? Junior asked. "That'll be pretty."

"Well, well," said the Captain, "he won't need to walk all the way. Somebody will pick him up on the road. All he needs is to get out of the woods. Can you do it?"

"I can make it," Homer said. "I'll be back as quick as I can. What time is it?"

"How the hell do I know what time it is, Homer?" Junior asked.

"Do I look like I'm wearing a watch? Does he?" The Captain smiled and shook his head.

•••••

Homer walked out through the woods in about an hour. He was cold when he started, but he soon felt warm. He reached the dirt road where they'd come in the night before and found the car gone. The side of the road was full of stones that hurt his feet, but the middle was smooth. Homer walked there. On either side were fir trees and birches and dusty, dry ferns beside the road.

Around every turn in the road Homer looked ahead. He expected to find Junior's car pulled over to the side, with Daisy and Becky waiting for him. They might be sleeping. He also expected every minute to find his clothes folded neatly by the side of the road where he couldn't miss them. It didn't happen. The car turned up three days later in a public parking lot at JFK Airport in New York. The case of Jameson's was in the trunk. Neither Homer nor Junior nor the Captain ever saw his clothes again.

The sun was on the road where Homer walked. He felt the air on his back and curiously on his crotch and thighs. The Captain had said he wouldn't have to walk all the way to town like that. Homer had had long, troubled dreams in which he walked naked into the village. The streets were full of people he knew, but they didn't seem to see him. But they might. At any moment the people might turn and discover him passing naked before them: that was the dream. But he was far from the village now; he wouldn't have to go in there. Out here it was easy. He was a man walking naked through the woods, over the hills, over the fallen trees and through the brush, walking naked like a deer, no more naked than a deer, no less. He came to the blacktop, went right, and walked at the edge of the pavement back the way they had come the night before, the way to the farmhouses, Curry's, and home. He hadn't gone half a mile when he heard a car coming behind him. Homer walked on a little, and when he knew the car was approaching he turned to face it. He held up his hand.

The Women at Holiday's

IT WAS HOMER PATCH, the second constable, who drove out toward Dead River Settlement because Valentine didn't want to. "You might as well go ahead," Valentine said. "She's called, twice, Gertrude, Gretchen—whatever her name is. She's got the whing-whangs. She says somebody is, what, living in her barn? I don't know. I'm sick of listening to her, I know that."

"I'm blocked," Homer said.

"Well, move it, then," Valentine said.

They were at the firehouse. Valentine's car was out front. He could have got in and driven right off, but they had to move the fire-truck so Homer could get out. When he got backed around and out on the road, he could see Valentine in the rearview, waving him off. Valentine had to be the boss.

Homer drove through the village and took the north road. Noon-time in the last of May: on either side shade trees in the walls were blowing white, and the old apple trees, white and some pink. Homer went over the bridge and out along the river. On his right a kid on a tractor was skidding logs out of the woods and into the old mowing beside the road. It might have been Fairbrother's big kid. They were cutting timber up in the woods above the mowing. Homer could hear the saws. The kid was pulling the logs down to where the truck from the mill could get them. Homer turned right, onto the road that led to Dead River Settlement.

Before the war there had been three farms on the Dead River road: Littlejohn's, St. Just's, and the last farm, Holiday's, set right back under the mountain where the road ended. Littlejohn had sold, Just's had burned, and Holiday had died, ten, twelve years ago, and left nobody. Holiday had been sick for years and hadn't really worked the place since Homer could remember, since Homer was a kid himself. Two women from Boston bought Holiday's house and land. They used the place for summers. They were women in their fifties, early sixties. They kept to themselves. One, Trowbridge, the little, jumpy one: a librarian? A schoolteacher? Gretel Trowbridge. The other, the big one, Liszt, was a different kind of thing. She looked like a prizefighter. Bernadette Liszt. That one wouldn't give you the time of day. It was possible she had gone away, though. She hadn't been around at all last year, at least she hadn't been seen. Had she taken off? Had she gone? Valentine wouldn't be sorry. They didn't get on.

Since all three farms out the Dead River road had been given up, the pastures and mowings had grown over, and now the women's house was a couple of miles from nothing, out in the woods. Grass grew faintly in the middle of the road, and branches slapped the sides of Homer's car and squeaked like long fingernails along the roof as he passed. He missed the place at first. He drove right by the house and had to turn around at the dead end. When he came up the driveway beside the house, Gretel Trowbridge was in the door, and before he was out of his car she was at his window.

"Mr. Patch," she said. "I called Tuesday and then twice yesterday, but Mr. Valentine took no interest. Mr. Patch, what if my house had been on fire?"

"Your house wasn't on fire," Homer said. He turned off his car's engine. "If it had been, they would have come right off," he said through the open car window. "Do you want to step back, now?"

"Summer residents are citizens, too, Mr. Patch," Gretel said. "We pay taxes. We are entitled to protection, even if we are not everybody's cousins."

"Do you want to step back, now?" Homer said. "So I can get the door open and get out? Then we can see what you've got here." Gretel took two steps back but kept her eye fast on Homer. He got out of the car and stood, settling his belt, looking around.

They didn't much keep the place up: a was-white house now the color of an old stone except over darker patches where the walls were wet; a rusty screen door; at the corner of the house a big old lilac, tall as the second-story windows but full of dead branches; grass not mowed and grown up with dandelions and the little blue flowers like, what, daisies, that come in the mowings; up top, a shake roof that ought to have been replaced thirty years ago and daylight visible through the chimney. There wasn't any reason somebody couldn't have come out when she called Tuesday.

"Do you want to show me?" Homer asked.

He followed her back of the house, around the barn, and then down hill into the woods. Gretel Trowbridge led him down along a rocky pathway where water must have run earlier in the spring, past wet ferns and green branches. Ahead of them the little hill leveled out, and at the bottom was a low, unpainted shed sitting right in the woods, with trees and brush growing up to its walls and no clearing except directly in front of the door where the path they were on led. The building wasn't a hundred feet from the house and barn, but they were out of sight because of the hill and the thick woods all around.

"Wait," Gretel said when she and Homer reached the shed. She went to the door and knelt beside it. Then she turned to Homer and beckoned him.

"You see?" she said.

She pointed at the doorway, and Homer saw a single white thread hanging at knee height from a nail in the left-hand doorframe. Gretel picked up the hanging end and untied it from the nail. From her pocket she took a new spool of white thread. She took a piece four feet long from the spool, tied one end to the nail, and drew the thread tight across the doorway to another nail in the right doorframe, where she wound the end around and around to hold it. She stood up and pointed to the white thread stretched across the door.

"My trap," Gretel said. "It was broken. The thread was broken. That means somebody has been in the door. Through the door. He broke the thread. I set the thread across the door last night, and now it's broken, as you see it. I did the same the night before. Somebody has used the door, or the thread would still be up. Do you see, Mr. Patch?"

"Yes," Homer said.

Gretel bent to untie the thread and let it hang beside the doorway. Then she opened the plank door of the shed. "There's more," she said.

The shed inside was a room eight by fifteen feet. Holiday had built it as a sugarhouse, but since his time somebody had taken away the fire arch and let windows into the walls to fit the shed out for living. In the middle of the room were a plain table and a hard chair, and opposite the door, in a corner under the window, was a bed. Or, not a real bed, Homer saw, but a platform seven or eight inches high that you could put a mattress on but that now was bare boards. Along one wall was a rack of clothes, women's clothes, more than you could ever wear, all kinds: dresses, gowns, shawls, long coats, short coats, capes—rich clothes like, what, velvet, satin, and their colors the same: scarlet, green, black, and purple. Some were fur or trimmed in fur. The rack of clothes went all along the end of the little room, from one corner to the other, like clothes in a store, but not new clothes: old clothes, and full of dust.

"Here," said Gretel. She went to the bed and picked up from the floor beside it an empty quart beer bottle. She gave it to Homer and showed him that there were dead cigarette butts inside the bottle. "And here," Gretel said. She got down on the floor and pulled from under the bed an empty box that had held fried chicken, a torn candy wrapper, a stump of candle, and a pair of large, black, nearly worn-out man's leather boots.

"There has been someone in this room. Living, or staying here, Mr. Patch," Gretel said.

"Yes," Homer said. "Yesterday, was it, you found this stuff?"

Gretel got up from the floor. She dusted off her knees and stood for a moment beside Homer. "I only got up here to the farm Friday night," she said. "Saturday I was opening the house. Sunday I cleaned. Monday I came down here for the first time. I found what you saw. And I could smell him, whoever had been here. I could smell his cigarettes, and I could smell *him*. I sleep in here, sometimes, you see," she said.

Homer nodded.

"I called the constable then," Gretel went on. "Nobody came, as I told you. I spoke to Mr. Valentine, then I spoke to his wife. I called twice Tuesday. Now you've come, Mr. Patch, you've seen, and I want to know what you're going to do."

The farm, Homer was thinking. *I got up to the farm,* she had said.

Did they call the place "the farm"? Did they think it was a farm? It was no farm. It had been a farm, but it was no farm now.

"Your clothes?" he asked.

"They belong to my friend," Gretel said. "I keep them for her. She's been away."

"I hadn't seen her," Homer said. "Some while."

"No," Gretel said. "She's traveling."

Homer nodded. He looked at her.

"But she'll be back," Gretel said.

Homer nodded again.

"She is coming back," said Gretel Trowbridge.

She stood in the doorway waiting for Homer. For a moment they looked together at the interior of the shed, the bed, the table, the dark roof and rafters above, the line of garments on their rack, the place where Holiday's fire arch had been.

"This was a saphouse," Homer said. "Sugarhouse, it was."

•••••

Outside, Gretel shut the door and turned to Homer.

"Well, Mr. Patch?" she said.

"Don't you do up your line?" Homer asked her. Gretel hadn't tied the thread across the door when they left the shed.

What?" Gretel asked.

"It seems as though you'd do up your line, your string, there, the way you had it," Homer said.

"Not till tonight," she said. "That's when he comes. What should I do, Mr. Patch?" They stood before the shed.

"Get a lock for this door, here, I would," Homer said. "Padlock would do."

"Oh, Mr. Patch," Gretel said. She laid her hand on the door and rattled it.

"Anyone could get in here, whether it was locked or not," she said. "The door isn't strong, and the windows don't have locks."

"Anyone could get in," Homer said. "But most probably they wouldn't. Something about a locked door. See, whoever has been here is just some guy drifting through. Some kid. A runaway, it might be. There are a lot of them lately. They sleep in barns, in the woods. Kids. We see a good many of them the last, I guess, three, four years. They move on. There's no real harm in them. They might steal out of your garden, but you don't have a garden. You lock the shed, whoever it is most probably will leave you alone."

Gretel looked at Homer for a minute when he had finished. "No, Mr. Patch," she said at last. "That is not good enough. You agree with me that there is some man, some intruder, living on my property, and when I am able, after no small effort, to get your office to respond in the first place, you refuse to do anything about it. You tell me to get a lock for the door. That is not what I am waiting to hear from you, Mr. Patch. I am waiting to hear what you are going to do to protect me and my property from the intruder we both know is here."

"What do you want me to do?" Homer asked her.

"Well," Gretel said. "Come here. Tonight. Stay here, and when he comes, then take him. Arrest him. Take him away. You can do that, can't you? You have that authority."

"Maybe," Homer said.

"Are you armed?" she asked.

"What?" Homer asked. "You mean with a gun? No."

He looked at her, looked around at the woods, the shed, the path to the house.

"See what it is you're asking me," he said. "You want me to come here and, what, shoot some kid for using your shed to get in out of the rain. That's what it comes to. You want to make a lot of trouble here that needn't be. My advice to you is what I said: lock the door. He will move on, and you won't be bothered. There's no need to bring in an army out here for something like this."

"I don't want an army, Mr. Patch," Gretel said. "I only want you."

Homer sighed. "Could I get a glass of water?" he asked.

Gretel turned and started back up the path to the house. Homer waited in front of the shed. When he couldn't see her any longer, he went around the shed to the back. There the woods went gently down hill to a brook, and the trees and underbrush were thick and green. Homer walked away from the rear of the shed and into the woods a little way, then he stopped and looked out into the trees.

"Hugh?" he said.

"Hugh?" Homer said again, a little louder. "Hugh, you hearing this, Hugh? You there?"

Homer listened, but there was no sound from the woods except birds, and not many of them.

He turned to go back around to the front of the shed. From where he stood he could see through the rear windows the room within. He went up to one of the windows. Inside the shed the dark, florid clothes hanging on their rack went down the side of the room like an army passing: a file of square shoulders, straight backs. What was she, the other one, this one's friend, to have so many clothes? Were they like costumes? Was she some kind of an actress? "Man-hater," Valentine had called her.

Valentine hated Bernadette Liszt because, some years before, he had tried to blow one by her, and she hadn't let him. Only a little one. When the two women bought Holiday's place, there was junk in the house and in the yard that they wanted carted away: old newspapers, a busted chair, a bed, a bathtub, Holiday's old iron kitchen range, axles and fenders from two of Holiday's cars. Bernadette Liszt hired Valentine to come with his truck and a helper to take Holiday's junk to the dump. Valentine got Homer, and they collected the stuff in one trip. It might have taken them half an hour. Then Valentine sent Bernadette and Gretel a bill for $100.

The next morning Bernadette drove into the firehouse lot and stopped her car in front of the bay. She was alone. She got out, left the door open and the engine running. Homer was cleaning the firetruck.

"Where's your boss?" Bernadette asked Homer.

"My boss?" Homer said.

"What's his name. Valentine," Bernadette said. "Where's Valentine?"

"In back," Homer said. Bernadette walked past him into the firehouse. She held in her hand the piece of paper that was the bill Valentine had sent. Homer followed her.

Valentine was sitting behind his desk. Bernadette stood in front of him and showed him the bill.

"This was a mistake, right? This number? A hundred dollars?" Bernadette asked him.

Valentine took the bill, looked at it, handed it back to her. "No mistake," Valentine said.

"Yes, it was," Bernadette said. "You tried to hold us up. That was a mistake. What do you think we are? What do you think you are? Do you know what you are?"

"Wait a minute," Valentine said.

"Stupid," Bernadette said. "You're stupid. You're big, and you're stupid. Don't you ever, ever try to do us like that again. Ever. Do you hear me?"

"Now, wait a minute," Valentine began, and he got to his feet, but Bernadette leaned across his desk, hooked a finger in his belt, and shoved Valentine's bill down the front of his pants. Then she dropped two five-dollar bills on the desk, turned, and walked out of the firehouse.

Valentine pulled the piece of paper out of his pants. He didn't touch the money on his desk. He looked at Homer.

"Temper on her," Valentine said.

Homer watched Bernadette Liszt get into her car and drive away.

"Man-hater," Valentine said. "Looking like she does, she can't get a man, is her trouble."

"I wouldn't have said she'd wanted one," Homer said.

"What the hell do you think you know about it?" Valentine said.

In the woods back of the shed, Homer heard Gretel Trowbridge coming with his water. He left the window to go meet her in front of the shed, and when he came around he found her with a glass of water in one hand and in the other an old-fashioned shotgun so big it looked as though it belonged on wheels.

"Listen," Homer said.

"Have your water, Mr. Patch," Gretel said. She handed him the glass.

"Thank you," Homer said. He drank a little water.

"Is that loaded?" he asked.

"It is," Gretel said.

Homer took another drink of water. "You had best let me take that," he said.

"Oh, no, Mr. Patch," Gretel said. "I need it. You won't act to protect me, so I need this to protect myself. And I will use it. Make no mistake."

"That thing belongs in a museum," Homer told her. "If you tried to fire it, it could blow up in your face."

"If so, then my troubles would probably be over, wouldn't they?" Gretel said. "Shall we go back?"

She took the water glass from Homer's hand and led the way back up the woods path. At the house they stopped by Homer's car. Gretel set the empty glass on the car's fender and stood with the stock of the shotgun on her toe and the barrel pointing up at her chin.

"Hold it away," Homer said. He took the gun in Gretel's hands and gave it to her to hold so it pointed up and off her shoulder.

"Is that better, Mr. Patch?" Gretel asked. "Is your mind eased?"

"You'd better give that to me to keep for now," Homer said.

"You can have it, Mr. Patch," Gretel said. "If you'll promise to come back tonight and help me with whoever is intruding. Otherwise, not."

"I don't know if I will or not," Homer said.

"Then I'll keep my protection," Gretel said. "Until you make up your mind."

Homer got into his car and started the engine. "You're not the one needs protection," he said, but Gretel couldn't hear him for the noise of the car.

"What did you say, Mr. Patch?" she asked.

"It ain't you that needs protection," Homer said.

"You know perfectly well what's going on here, don't you, Mr. Patch?" Gretel asked.

"Do I?" Homer said.

"You know who's been in my shed," Gretel said. "You know who it is. Don't you?"

"No," Homer said.

Gretel gave him a thin smile. Her first. Her last.

"Tell him." Gretel said. "Tell him that if he comes back tonight and I'm alone, I will shoot him."

She lifted the shotgun in her hands.

"All right," Homer said. "I'll come back if I can. I don't promise when or how long for. Now, you don't do anything until you hear from me. I'll either call up or come, one of the two. Do you understand?"

"I understand I can protect myself if you aren't here to do your job," Gretel said.

Homer backed his car out of the driveway and got it straightened out in the road. At the house Gretel still stood with the shotgun at port arms. How did she come to have a gun like that? Must be it had been Holiday's gun. Must be it had been in the house with the rest of Holiday's things when the women bought the place. Homer put the car in gear and drove away.

Down the road, the house behind him, Homer slowed so he could look into the woods, but the trees and brush were so thick and green that the shed wasn't visible. Years back, you could see it from here, when Holiday boiled his sap in the shed in late winter. A whole gang of them would come out to help. March time, with the snow going and the trees black and shiny like seals. At sugaring the women would pour hot syrup right out of the pan onto snow for the kids to eat, and one year, when Homer was a little kid, they'd made it too hot and he'd burned his tongue. He'd cried then, and his sister Caroline had taken him outside and given him a pickle to suck on. Then Holiday himself had come out of the saphouse and seen Homer, crying, being comforted by his sister.

"What's this?" Holiday had shouted. "What's he, a baby? *Oh boohoo- hoo, boo-hoo.* What are you, a baby? Be a man."

"You shut up," Caroline had told him.

"What did you say to me?" Holiday asked her.

"I told you to shut up," Caroline said. "I'll tell you again: you shut up, you dirty old drunk."

And Holiday had shut up. He went past Homer and Caroline to the group of men standing off from the saphouse in the muddy snow. The men were passing a pint of something among them. One of them laughed, but it wasn't Holiday. Caroline had put it right to him that day. Some things didn't change. Nobody came over Caroline—not then, not now. Homer had been what, six? Seven? Forty years ago, close to it. His big sister, Caroline.

He had driven two miles at least from the house when he saw that the water glass Gretel had set on his fender was miraculously still there, rattling, but the same moment he saw it, it fell off.

•••••

When Homer had gone, Gretel Trowbridge, still carrying the shotgun walked back around the barn, into the woods, and down the path to the shed. She let herself in by the door where the white thread hung uselessly. Inside, Gretel leaned the shotgun in a corner. The gun was empty. She had told Homer the gun was loaded. It was not loaded. She didn't so much as know how to load it, and if she had, she would never fire at a man for taking shelter in her shed.

When she and Bernadette had cleaned out the house, the shotgun had been with the other junk of Holiday's. Gretel had carried it down from the upstairs. She had been taking it out to the pile they were making in the yard.

"We'll keep that," Bernadette had said.

"This?" Gretel said. "What for? What need?"

"We'll keep it," Bernadette said.

"I don't see why," Gretel said.

"Keep it," Bernadette said.

Gretel sat on the bed, raised her feet, and lay out on her back. Above her in the darkness of the roof, the rafters went up to the peak.

She thought she would rest for an hour. She lay on the hard, uncovered bed. She would not close her eyes. He wouldn't come while she was in here. But he wouldn't know until he found her. To be safe she should put the thread back across the door. But the thread wouldn't keep him out. The thread would prove he had been in, but it wouldn't keep him out. Only strength could do that, only power, and of power she had so little. And then, she was alone.

That constable, that man. He wanted Gretel to believe the visitor was a runaway, a waif, a motherless child, one of the children of the storm. How absurd. Did he know better, himself? Of course he did. Had he lied to her to protect someone he knew? Of course he had. But she had done the same. She had done the same.

She is coming back.

"They despise you," Bernadette had said. "Despise them."

No.

•••••

Homer drove back the way he had come until he reached the place where the Dead River road joined the road to the village. There he pulled to the side and stopped. He sat. He rested his hands on the steering wheel and looked out at the road in front of him.

What was she up to with that string across the door? It was a trick, a trap. What for? You don't need a trick to tell you somebody has been in. You look and see he has. It's a good trick but it doesn't tell you anything you didn't know without it and it doesn't change anything. Still, it's something she can do, something to look like she's helping herself. Nobody else has been helping her.

When Homer had been sitting in his car for ten minutes, a truck came down the road from the direction of the village and stopped. It was Wilson Speed's truck. Hugh was riding in the back. When Wilson stopped, Hugh thumped on the roof of the cab and jumped down from the truck. Wilson got going again, leaving Hugh in the road. Hugh began to walk toward the Dead River road. He saw Homer waiting. Hugh stopped, looked up the road after Wilson's truck going away, then walked on toward Homer. Homer opened the passenger's door of his car when Hugh came up. Hugh got in beside him.

"If it ain't the constable," Hugh said.

"How long have you been up to the saphouse at Holiday's?" Homer asked him.

Hugh looked at Homer for a minute, then turned and faced the car's front. He and Homer sat and looked out at the road together.

"I don't know," Hugh said. "Couple of nights. He kicked me out, home. More than a couple. Might be four, five nights. He kicked me right out."

"I heard," Homer said. "You had another fight, he said. In town, was it, he said?"

"*Aww,*" said Hugh, "it was only a little fight."

"You have a court date down there?" Homer asked.

"No court," Hugh said. "No trouble. The way I said: it was no big deal fight."

"Must be that's why they put you in the lockup for the night," Homer said. "It don't matter: you're all done at Holiday's. Go home, or find someplace else, one of the two."

"Who says I'm all done?" Hugh asked.

"The lady found your stuff," Homer said. "She's there now. You're all done."

"Why?"

"Well," Homer said. "One thing, you're trespassing. Then, too, she's got an old duck gun up there, and she's waiting for you right now."

"A gun?" Hugh said. "Golly, Mr. Constable, you're like to scare me to death."

"Stay clear of Holiday's, now," Homer said.

"Who's going to make me?" Hugh asked.

Across the road that they faced was an old pasture, and a hundred yards farther, across the pasture, pine woods and the river, running here at the edge of the cleared land, a little way into the woods. No cows used the place any more. There would be broken-down fence at the far edge, Homer knew, that had kept the cows out of the woods. The trees along there would be full of rusty barbed wire, staples, and nails that had held the fence. Nobody would ever cut those trees, or nobody who knew better, because the old iron deep within them would wreck the saw.

"Who's going to make me?" Hugh asked. "Valentine? You got that fat fool Valentine hiding in the trunk, here, in case things get rough? I hope so. I'd like for him to try and make me. I'd like that real good."

"Not Valentine," Homer said.

Homer extended his right arm along the back of the seat between him and Hugh. He put his hand on Hugh's neck, behind, gently, and pushed Hugh's head and upper body forward. Hugh started to resist, he started to push back against Homer's hand. Then he didn't. Homer bore Hugh slowly down and held him by the back of the neck.

"You know?" Homer said. "They call it the farm. The women up there. *The farm*, is what they call the place now."

Hugh didn't answer him. His forehead was against the dashboard of Homer's car and Homer's hand held him there.

"It ain't a farm," Homer said. "It was. Holiday farmed. But it ain't a farm now. Because on a farm, the animals, they breed. The cows, horses, pigs, the chickens, the rest. They get together. They breed. That's what a farm is: breeding. Two women by themselves, like they are, can't breed. Can they? They can't get together to breed, so they can't have a farm. It ain't a farm any more."

"There's only the one, anyhow," Hugh said.

"What?" Homer said. He let go Hugh's neck. Hugh sat up. He leaned back on his seat, shut his eyes.

"There's only one of them up there," Hugh said. "Not two."

"That's right," Homer said. "There's only the one. She's all alone up there. And if you go back—tonight, tomorrow, any time at all—I'll know. I'll know, and it won't be Valentine you'll be talking to."

"Okay," Hugh said.

"Not Valentine," Homer said. "You understand?"

"Okay," Hugh said.

Homer started the car.

"I'll drop you, home," he said.

"No," Hugh said. "You don't need to. I can get a ride. I can walk."

"Don't be afraid," Homer said. "This part's over now. Sure, I'll drop you. I'm going right by. I'm going by the hardware."

•••••

Later that afternoon, when Homer got back up to Holiday's, he didn't wait on Gretel Trowbridge. He left his car in the driveway where he had left it earlier and went right down to the sugarhouse. He didn't see Gretel. She was in the house, probably.

Homer had brought with him a new lock-set, a padlock, a screwdriver, and a little push-drill. He set them down and knelt before the door to the sugarhouse. Gretel's white thread hung by its nail in the doorframe. Homer let it hang. He laid out his tools. Eight screws: four for the strap, four for the ring. He marked the holes. The old pine boards, he found, were soft. He hardly needed his drill. In ten minutes he was done. He hung the lock on the ring and got to his feet. Gretel stood behind him, watching him work.

"Mr. Patch," she said.

"There you go," Homer said. He snapped the padlock shut over the ring. He had the key. Two keys. He handed them to Gretel.

"There you go," Homer said. "You're all set now."

Gretel took the keys, looked at them. She shook her head.

"How do you know?" she asked.

"I told you," Homer said. "Keep it locked up and they get the idea. You won't have any more trouble here."

"If so, Mr. Patch," Gretel said. "It won't be because of this." She held up the keys to the padlock. "It will be because you decided to act. Are you staying now, as I asked?"

"No," Homer said. "No need. Nobody will come."

"You know who has been here, don't you, Mr. Patch?" Gretel asked. "You have known from the first."

"Yes," Homer said.

"And what did you do?" Gretel asked.

"I talked to him," Homer said. "He won't be back."

"I'm much obliged to you, then, Mr. Patch," Gretel said. "But in the event, I don't see why I need the lock."

"You need something," Homer said. "What have you got? That string? That won't do the job. You know it won't."

"No," Gretel said. "No, I don't suppose it will, will it?"

Homer picked up his tools. He was ready to leave now. Four o'clock in the afternoon, and broad day at this time of the year, but in the woods around Holiday's old sugarhouse the shadows advanced, the evening advanced.

"You're sure, Mr. Patch?" Gretel said. "You're certain he—whoever it was you spoke to—is gone?"

"I'm sure," Homer said. "He's gone and he won't be back."

Gretel nodded. She looked around her at the trees, the woods, the dark distances farther into the woods, the old boards of the sugarhouse, the old door, the bright steel of the new hardware fixed onto the door. She nodded.

"He's not the only one," she said.

•••••

"Where have you been?" Valentine asked.

"At Holiday's" Homer said.

"That's right," Valentine said. "What was it she wanted? Somebody in her barn?"

"Calhoun's kid," Homer said. "He'd been sleeping there. Calhoun kicked him out again. He'd gone up to Holiday's, was sleeping in the saphouse."

"Is that right?" Valentine said. "So what did you do?"

"Talked to the kid. Told him to get off," Homer said.

"You were gone since eleven o'clock," Valentine said. "It's on for five. Doing that took you all afternoon?"

"I went back up there," Homer said. "I got a lock to her door so people can't walk right in that way. I got the lock, got my tools, went back, put the lock on, up there."

"How much for the lock?" Valentine asked.

"Six bucks," Homer said.

"I hope you don't think that's on the office," Valentine said. "That's your treat."

"I know," Homer said.

"What about that other one?" Valentine asked. "That bullfighter buddy of hers. See her, did you?"

"No," Homer said. "She's moved away. She don't live there any more."

"Is that right?" Valentine said. "Damn shame. She was a real asset, that one."

Homer looked at him.

"Yeah," Valentine said. "Well, but you got everything squared away for her up there, did you?"

"Pretty much," Homer said.

The Montreal Express

THE TOWN CLERK, AGNES MACKENZIE, came into the little meeting room in the rear of the building and shut the door behind her. "I'm glad somebody's here," she said. "I think we have a problem."

At the conference table in the middle of the room, the sheriff's deputy was listening to the radio. He held up his hand.

"Can it wait?" the deputy said. "I want to hear this."

The deputy's name was Rackstraw. His first name was Norman, but everyone called him Buddy—young Buddy Rackstraw.

He turned the radio up. A big storm was moving down that morning from Canada. It had been snowing in Burlington since midnight, in Montpelier since dawn, and it had started an hour since in St. Johnsbury. The snow, once it came, would fall all that day, the radio said, all that night. It would snow a foot and a half, two feet, more than that in the mountains.

"It's going to be a pisser," said Buddy Rackstraw.

"What is it, Ag?" Homer Patch asked Agnes. Homer, the town constable then, was back there too.

"Come on," Buddy said. "I said wait, okay? I told you to hold it a second."

He leaned toward the radio on the table. The little room behind the Town Clerk's office didn't have windows; the storm might have come already. It might be snowing outdoors this minute.

"It's started in White River," Buddy said. "It's going to be some pisser."

"Ag?" Homer asked.

"A man is out here wants the birth certificate for Racer St. Just," Agnes said.

"Racer?" Homer said.

"Racer?" Buddy said. He turned the radio off.

"Nobody you know?" Homer asked Agnes.

Agnes shook her head.

"Racer?" Buddy said.

"Does he say he's Racer?" Homer asked Agnes.

"No. He put down five dollars. He wants a copy of the birth certificate. Attested copy."

Homer nodded. He looked around the little room: twelve by fifteen, no windows, the one door, electric clock high on the wall, two steel cabinets, the table and six wooden chairs for the selectmen's meetings. Racer St. Just had died—what? Three years earlier? Four?—in a motorcycle crash on the highway.

"You ought to get them to run you a phone line in here, Ag," Homer said.

"They talked about it," Agnes said.

"What does some guy want with Racer?" Buddy asked.

"What does he want?" Agnes said. "I told you. He wants his birth certificate."

"Well, give it to him," Buddy said. "He paid."

"No, Buddy," Agnes said. "He wants his, he wants Racer's papers. He wants his, you know, his documents."

"He wants his name," Homer said.

"Say what?" Buddy asked.

"Buddy," Agnes said. "He wants Racer's papers, you know? He wants to use Racer's name. If he's got an attested certificate of birth for Racer, he can get whatever else he needs. He can get a social security card, a driver's license. He can get a passport. He can be Racer."

"He can like hell," Buddy said. "Not in my town, he can't."

"Buddy," Agnes said.

"Is the guy by himself?" Buddy asked her.

"Yes," Agnes said.

"Well, okay," said Buddy. "Okay." He stood up, but Homer kept his seat at the table.

"Have you got anybody else out there now, Ag?" Homer asked.

"Wilson," Agnes said.

"Where is the guy?" Homer asked. "And where is Wilson?"

"Where are they?" Agnes said. "They're right out there."

"I mean where are they located at," Homer said. "Where are they in the room?"

"Oh," said Agnes. "Well, let's see: the guy? The guy is at the counter, uh, at my cash register. Kind of in the corner next to the wall? Wilson? Wilson is sitting on the bench."

"Okay, then," Buddy said. "Okay, then, Homer?"

Homer stood up. "You might wait in here, Ag," he said.

"I'll go along," Agnes said.

Buddy, standing at the table, touched his belt. "My weapon's in the cruiser, you know," he said. "I ought to worn it, but I left it in the cruiser."

"Best place for it," Homer said.

•••••

The Town Clerk's office was divided by a counter that ran three quarters the length of the room. In front of the counter, near the door to the outside, Wilson Speed waited on a wooden bench set against the wall. The other man was in front of him and to his left, standing at the counter. When Agnes, Homer, and Buddy Rackstraw left the back room and came into the office, the man watched them. He watched Agnes take her place across the counter from him and he watched Homer cross the room toward Wilson, but Buddy was the one he kept his eyes on. Buddy was the last to leave the meeting room, and Buddy was the only one wearing the uniform of a law-enforcement officer.

Homer went around the end of the counter and spoke to Wilson. He ignored the man at the counter.

"Big one coming," Homer said.

"I guess," Wilson said.

"It going to snow two feet, you think?" Homer asked.

"They say," Wilson said.

"I hope not," Homer said. "Friday afternoon? Roads full of people coming up for the weekend? They'll be all over the map."

"Their lookout," said Wilson. "They might try staying home."

"Their lookout, and mine," Homer said. "And his," meaning Buddy, who now stood at the end of the counter, behind Homer. Homer turned toward Buddy and for the first time faced the man at the other end of the counter.

He had shifted his place a little so he faced them, his left side against the counter. Dark. Not bad looking, in a way: age hard to tell, but not young, no kid, no Buddy Rackstraw. Oh, no, not this one. This one's a different kind of thing. Tall, another half-head above Homer but thirty pounds lighter. Thin as a cord. Fancy gray overcoat with the middle button fastened to hold it closed at his waist. Black hair, long, slicked straight back from his forehead, dark skin, and wide brown eyes. Not bad eyes, not mean, but what were they? Sad. Sad eyes.

Homer made a little move. He stepped to his left, putting himself between the man at the counter and Wilson Speed and opening more space between himself and Buddy. The man didn't turn with him. He never took his eyes off Buddy, but when Homer moved the man put his right hand inside his overcoat and left it there. Homer stopped where he was. He could have come to the man in three steps. Too many.

Buddy came around the corner.

"Can I help you, sir?" Buddy asked the man.

"Help me?"

"It's a certificate of birth you're looking for?" Buddy asked.

"That's right."

"For St. Just, Pascal?" Buddy asked. He took a step closer to the other.

The man nodded. His hand was inside his coat. He waited for Buddy.

"Can I see some I.D., sir?" Buddy asked. He held out his hand and started toward the man, but Homer said, "Wait a minute, Buddy."

"Stay where you are, soldier," the man at the counter said. Buddy stopped.

"Good," the man said.

"Oh, my God," Agnes Mackenzie said. "Homer?"

Homer looked at Buddy. "Take it easy," he told him. But Buddy was watching the other. Buddy was close enough to him to make a move. Buddy's shoulders rose an inch, and gathered. Homer stepped to Buddy's side and took hold of his left arm above the elbow. He lifted Buddy a little, so Buddy's left foot came off the floor and he leaned into the counter. "Easy," Homer said.

"Come on," Buddy said. "Come on, what are you doing?"

"He's doing good, soldier," the man said. "Listen to him. Listen to the big guy. He knows. He's the best friend you ever had."

"What is this?" Wilson Speed asked. He was still sitting on the bench. "What is going on here?"

"Please," Agnes said. She stood opposite the man, with both her hands lying flat on the counter in front of her. "Please," she said.

"Think about it," the man said. "Is it worth somebody getting hurt? No, it isn't. Everybody slow down." He spoke to Agnes. "Who else is in the back room, there?"

"Nobody," Agnes said. "Nobody is there."

"What's in there?"

Homer let go of Buddy's arm so Buddy could stand on both feet in front of the counter. He left his hand on Buddy's shoulder. Buddy stayed put. The man's eyes never moved from him.

"Nothing," Agnes said. "Some files. Some chairs. You know. I don't know. Nothing."

"Alright," the other said. "The man sitting down over there, you want to get up and go on into the back room. Go ahead. Then her. Then the big guy. Then the soldier. Nobody moves fast. Nobody wants trouble."

Wilson Speed got up from the bench and walked toward the meeting room in the rear. Agnes followed him. Homer went after Agnes, then Buddy.

In the meeting room the four of them stood in a line against the wall opposite the door. The man came into the room only a little way.

He waited just inside the door. He hadn't taken his hand from inside his coat. He looked about the room.

"No phone?" he asked.

"No," said Agnes.

"Go ahead, sit down," the man said. "Not you," he said to Agnes.

"You come around here."

Agnes went around the conference table and stood before him.

Buddy, who had sat down in one of the chairs, started to get to his feet again.

"It's alright, Buddy," Agnes said.

She and the man now stood together at the door. Wilson Speed and Homer sat across the room on the opposite side of the long table. Beside Homer, Buddy was half out of his chair. Homer took him by the belt and pulled him back down.

"I'll be alright, Buddy," Agnes said.

"She and me are gone," the man said. "You sit in here. You got a clock up there. Give us ten minutes on the clock. Ten. Don't leave the room. Soldier? You hear this? You decide if she gets hurt, soldier. You, alright? Not me. You decide."

"What are you talking about?" Wilson said. "Do you think you can just leave us here? Do you think we'll just sit in here? There's no lock on that door. You can't lock it."

"She's the lock," the man said. He took a step back and let Agnes go before him out of the meeting room. He never took his hand out of his coat and he never took his eyes off Buddy, except at the last second, just before he closed the door on them, he looked at Homer. Not sad eyes, either, or not only, but—what? Patient. Patient eyes.

•••••

After the office door closed, Buddy, Homer, and Wilson Speed sat at the table. None of them spoke. How long? Not long. Then Buddy said, "Jesus, Homer," and Wilson said, "What in the world was that about?"

"Bad news," Homer said. "Bad news is what that was."

"Jesus, Homer," Buddy said. "I could have taken him. I don't think he even had a gun."

"He had one, alright," Wilson Speed said.

"I don't think he did," Buddy said. "Did you see it?"

"No," Wilson said.

"I had him," Buddy said. "What did you stop me for?"

"I stopped you because you didn't have a move," Homer said.

"Not in here, no, I know I didn't," Buddy said. "Out there, a minute ago, I did."

Homer shook his head.

"You were out of your league," he said. "He was something you don't know about. He was something you never saw before."

"And you did?" Buddy Rackstraw said. "Come on, Homer."

"What about Agnes?" Wilson Speed said.

"She's safe," Homer said.

"You hope she is," Buddy said. "What, are you just going to sit here?"

"That's right," Homer said. "You, too."

•••••

Presently Homer got up and went to the door. He opened the door and went out. Buddy followed him. Wilson Speed stayed behind. In the office Buddy went first to the telephone on Agnes's desk. He picked the phone up and listened, then he dialed a number and began talking.

Homer left the office and went outside. The morning was gray, unformed, the air filling up with gray. All about, the frozen ground, the bare trees across the road, were gray, the color of ashes. A little wind, not hard but steady, was blowing out of the north. Homer went around the building to the side where the cars were parked. His car was there, and Arthur's truck, and Buddy's sheriff's cruiser, white with a red stripe and the light on top. Agnes sat in the back of Buddy's cruiser, behind the grate. She was locked in. When she saw Homer she smiled at him. She shrugged her shoulders.

In the dirt beside the sheriff's car, tracks led to the road and away. Homer saw them and saw at the same moment that the tracks were left not in dirt, not in ash, but in snow, the first, thin gray dust of snow. He went to let Agnes out and a puff of snow hit his face stinging, like a handful of sand.

Bandit Poker

THE END OF IT WAS THAT A COUPLE OF YEARS LATER person or persons unknown broke into Condosta's and cleaned the place out. They didn't fool with the lock. They evidently used a sledgehammer to knock down the door. They took it all: the cameras, the short-wave, the TV, the weights, the rowing machine, the guns, the power tools, the pinball, the coins. They took Condosta's Lionel cars. Condosta's secret thing didn't stop them. They cleaned the place right out. So it's all in wanting something and knowing what you want. It's all in having an object in view, an intelligent object, an adult object even if a criminal one. The second, the successful assailants on Condosta's were grownups. They wanted his stuff. Kevin and Zipper were kids. All they wanted was trouble. Trouble.

Kevin and Zipper hadn't enough trouble, they thought. They wanted more. It was inevitable they'd take on Condosta's.

Trouble as an end in itself, then, as a way of life: finding trouble, getting into trouble, visiting trouble on others. Trouble was Kevin and Zipper's DNA, their profoundest, most irresistible structure, as for others religion, art, women, alcohol, narcotics, promotion, power. Trouble was their army, navy, air force, and marines. Stuck as they were in a rural backwater offering little room for mayhem, they found themselves in some danger of becoming dull. They repeated themselves, Kevin and Zipper did: car wrecks, fights; fights, car wrecks.

Imagine General Custer rattling around old Fort Lincoln, parading his troops, polishing his leather, polishing his brass. Bored, bored, bored. Kevin and Zipper needed a Little Big Horn.

•••••

Kevin and Zipper: what are they?

Not criminals, exactly. The criminal is part of an economy in a way Kevin and Zipper have no idea of being. Not madmen. Madmen have, after their fashion, thought things through. Kevin and Zipper don't think things through. They are simple souls. Kevin and Zipper are the bearers of the ancient male principle of destruction and self-destruction. They smash up, lay waste, defy with a kind of deep physical ease that is better than thought, better than free will. They make trouble the way the bull runs at the fence, the way the blood horse lifts his head to the wind. It's what they do because of what they are.

Kevin and Zipper are the trouble cavalry.

And therefore, to be sure, an anachronism. Kevin and Zipper belong in a museum, or, if there were such a place, in a zoo for dangerous ideas. By all means let them be seen, visited. Let them be admired. For is theirs not the same material, the same force that produces the beloved heroes of romance: Roland, Lancelot, Coeur de Leon, the vainglorious Custer himself? In a world founded on trouble, trouble's thoughtless cavaliers have a necessary place, an honorable place, a place of legends. In a world founded otherwise the necessity is gone, the honor is gone. Only the legends remain, and they are reduced to constables' reports, to the repetitious, digressive stories of the small towns and villages.

Thus, Kevin and Zipper's breaking into Condosta's.

•••••

Condosta, a man of some mystery. In fact a New York City policeman retired to the north country on partial disability. A cop, Condosta was, and like all cops everywhere, eager to spend his money on expensive toys. It was known that his place out the old Bible Hill road was full of every kind of equipment as well as valuable collections. The coin collection alone, Condosta had told Homer Patch, the second constable, who came to investigate the break-in, was valued at $10,000, and he had a case full of old model railroad cars which, he assured Homer, were worth twice that much.

"How much?" Homer asked him.

"Twenty grand," Condosta said. "Give or take."

"How many of them have you got?" Homer asked.

"You mean right now? Eighteen," Condosta said.

"Let's see," Homer said. "So that's like eleven hundred apiece?"

"That's right," said Condosta.

"Eleven hundred dollars for a plastic boxcar," Homer said.

"That's right," Condosta said.

They'd take care, Kevin and Zipper would, to smash those good, when they got in there. Just smash them, every one of them. To show.

To show what?

To show it wasn't money they wrought for, but something higher, finer.

Condosta's place was a made-over hunting camp. Of course he had the grounds wired up. He had God knows what alarms, electric eyes, tripwires. So what if he did? Condosta went off by six every morning to a first-shift job at the sunglasses factory in Brattleboro. He wasn't there during the day, and he lived alone. Well, not alone. Alone for people, but not alone—and that was what really put it right up to Kevin and Zipper. That was what made Condosta's place higher and finer, better than any car wreck, better than any fight. For Condosta had a dog out there, a guard dog, a thing about the size of a calf that looked like an alligator on stilts.

Big sucker. Take your arm right off.

The great dog patrolled around Condosta's, outside, when he was at work. You had to get by the dog. You had to put the dog on ice while you went in. Then you had to get by him again on your way out. How to do that took some thought. The rest was just shopping. Not shopping. In shopping you take something home with you. At Condosta's Kevin and Zipper will wreck the place, bust up his fancy stuff, but they aren't looking for value. Anything they steal, they'll soon throw into the ditch. Do you take them for thieves? Because they break and enter? Not at all. Put away your stereotypes, your bourgeois assumptions. Kevin and Zipper are not thieves. They are called by a note pitched far above the hearing of any thief. Kevin and Zipper are vandals.

Get it right.

And in either case, whatever they are, withhold your regret. Don't regret Kevin and Zipper.

They are not wasted. No dedication, no devotion like that of Kevin and Zipper to trouble is ever wasted. Kevin and Zipper have forsworn place, possessions, in time probably even liberty. They have forsworn love. Yes, they are chaste. They are oddly sexless. Kevin and Zipper know little of women. Their own sisters, girl cousins, nieces are placid, decent young women a little given to overweight who hold jobs, take care of their aged parents, and not infrequently marry well. They want nothing to do with Kevin and Zipper, and if they did, if one of those girls should make a move toward them, Kevin and Zipper would flee. They would gallop away. Trouble is their bride.

Spare your regret. Nobody is claiming these are failed statesmen, philosophers, pediatricians. Don't regret what else they might have been. Regret that, taking account of what they are, nobody knows any longer what to do with them.

•••••

Kevin and Zipper took a week to scope out Condosta's. They left their car along another road entirely and walked a mile through the woods to his place. They approached carefully. They lay in the brush at the edge of the clearing and watched the house.

Mornings at six, Condosta came out, then the dog. Not a bad looking dog, from a distance, but even from a distance you noticed, along with its size, that it had no frisk, no play in it like any other dog. They watched Condosta and the dog go to Condosta's truck. They watched the dog jump up into the back of the truck. Condosta had food for it in there, some kind of meat for the dog, like, what, somebody's arm? Somebody's leg? A baby? He gave it to the dog, who got down from the truck and began to eat. Condosta climbed into the truck and drove away.

All day, then, Kevin and Zipper watched the dog. It sat in the yard behind the house until the sun got around, when it went to the little front porch and lay there in the shade. From time to time it got up and walked around the house. If a squirrel ran across the yard, a bird, even a deer, the dog didn't move, but if a branch fell in the woods on the other side of the house, or if you tossed a stick, it was there in two seconds. That was quite a dog Condosta had. It seemed to be everywhere at once. It had the whole place covered. The thing had moves that were not far short of supernatural: wherever you looked for it, it was there. If the dog was sleeping on Condosta's porch and Kevin and Zipper crept around to watch from the back of the house, the dog would be waiting for them. If they came at the house one day from a new direction or at a new time, it would meet them. However they approached, whenever, Condosta's dog would be there, standing in the yard, not able to see them up in the woods, but knowing them all the same, its legs stiff, its pointed ears cocked.

Condosta returned, usually, around four in the afternoon. He took the dog into the house with him. Then Kevin and Zipper went back through the woods to where they had left their car.

For a week they came to Condosta's, lay in the woods, watched, tried to fake Condosta's dog out, failed. They waited. They were patient.

Kevin and Zipper were patient.

Extraordinary.

Patience is not Kevin and Zipper's material. Patience is the antithesis of trouble. Patient? They? Kevin and Zipper, if one of their junker cars doesn't start on the third turn of the key, leap out, seize a wrecking bar, and smash all the windows. Kevin and Zipper, if their intimidated mothers set cold eggs before them, hurl the dish across the room, stamp out of the house. If the screen door, slammed furiously behind them, catches their heel, they whirl and rip it out of the frame. Kevin and Zipper's method is rage, not patience. They punch, they break, they wreck, they beat, but they do not wait and watch. That they are prepared to do so in the matter of Condosta's dog is a measure of their devotion.

It is as well a measure of their problem: Condosta's ubiquitous beast. The dog is onto them without even knowing they're out there. However they come, he's waiting for them. Trying to dodge Condosta's dog is like trying to surprise your reflection in a glass. They can't get around him. They're not about to take him head on. What they need now is a plan, but they may not know what a plan is.

•••••

Are these kids bad? You bet. Are they wicked, are they dangerous? Absolutely. What is it about them, then, that seems to inspire forgiveness, that seems to inspire protection? Is it that Kevin and Zipper act not for themselves? Is it that their dash after trouble is without self-interest—indeed, with the opposite of self-interest? The truth is, they are the ones they mostly injure. There is a free-floating quality to the trouble they make, an abstractness. Kevin and Zipper are the algebraic expression of youthful male trouble, itself a kind of mathematical function. It's a function, too, that takes on an enlarging life of its own in the equation that is society, like a compound interest, for there is more and more trouble as there are fewer and fewer ways to let off the kids who make trouble, the trouble cavalry, the Kevin-and-Zippers.

What do you do with them? Time was, when Kevin and Zipper made things too hot at home, they could light out for the territories, but the territories are gone. Then, of course, they used to die off more. Cholera was good, diphtheria, measles, but they're gone, too. The best solution was of course war: Roland, Lancelot, Coeur de Leon, Custer, Kevin, Zipper—feed those boys to the guns.

War.

We condemn it. We repudiate it. Maybe we are too hard on war.

•••••

How they decided to take care of Condosta's dog, the plan they at last made, which one thought of it, Kevin or Zipper? There is no knowing. They have about one human brain among them, which might as well be thought of as hovering in the air between their two heads, buzzing like a deerfly.

Terry Mackenzie had a truck with a cap: an enclosed bed and a door in the rear, like a little trailer. Kevin and Zipper would borrow the truck from Terry. They would run a wire from the door to the cab of the truck. They would drive right up to Condosta's when the dog was on guard. The dog would come to the truck. They wouldn't be able to get out with the dog right there, but because of the trick door they wouldn't have to. The door would be open. Inside, in the back of the truck, they'd have a piece of meat for the dog, the way Condosta had. The dog was used to that. He'd get up into the truck to get the meat, and Kevin and Zipper would haul on the wire and close the door. The dog would be in there. Condosta's place would be theirs. When they were ready to leave, they'd release the wire from the cab, the door would open, the dog would get out. Kevin and Zipper would be gone.

It works.

They did it. They waited for Condosta to leave and drove Terry's truck right up Condosta's lane and into his yard. The dog met them there. They backed the truck around, got it headed out. The dog came around the truck. In the rear Kevin and Zipper had two pounds of ground chuck. Sucker got a sniff of that, he was in there like a shot. Then, *bam*, Kevin was on the wire, slammed the door, held it. Zipper got out, ran around back, made the door fast. Division of labor, you see: first principle of peaceful human order, allowing mankind to advance to the social condition of the ant.

Condosta's was theirs.

The house was locked. Kevin had a little bar, about a foot long. He shoved it into the doorframe beside the lock, hit it with the heel of his hand to set it, then jerked it back. The lock popped open, and there they were. You can do much the same trick with an American Express card if you have one. Kevin and Zipper mostly pay cash, though.

They are in. They pause. A passage momentous, trembling, palpitating with danger, with disaster, with foolishness—as when the egregious General Custer, topping that grassy rise with his 200 troopers, saw spread before him in the valley the Indian encampment, 4000 strong, waiting for him—and cried, "Come on, lads, we've got them now!"

•••••

Inside Condosta's it was gloomy and close, with a dark smell like a cellar. There was a big room, a door, a set of steps leading up to a loft, another door behind the steps. Kevin and Zipper came into the middle of the main room, with the steps in front of them and on their left the little red and green lights of Condosta's pinball machine winking. The pinball machine said BANDIT POKER!

Bandit Poker?

Bandit Poker is about as far as they got, for as they stood in the middle of the room they heard a noise from behind and a second later Condosta's dog was coming through the open door and at them.

Kevin and Zipper didn't even get turned around to face it. Did they for an instant take the dog for another of Condosta's toys? A mechanical dog? Did they wonder how it had gotten out of Terry's truck, how their plan had failed? Did it occur to them that it hadn't failed, that Condosta had *two* dogs, the one they had locked in the truck, still there, and this one, its evil twin, now trying to chew Zipper's head off? Did they understand, in a crash of bright despair, that the reason why, during the past week, they had never been able to get around that dog was because there were two dogs, not one?

It leaped onto Zipper's back and drove him to the ground, where it fastened on the side of his throat. Zipper was screaming. Kevin kicked the dog in the side with his heavy boot. It gave a little yip but it kept working on Zipper. So Kevin reached around the dog's middle with his arms, picked it up, and threw it across the room. Kevin's big and strong, Zipper's a slight little kid. If the dog had taken Kevin down first rather than Zipper, the thing might have ended badly.

The dog hit the wall and fell to the floor stunned. Kevin got Zipper to his feet and half walked, half carried him out of there. There was a lot of blood. It spilled on the floor, it spilled on the earth of the yard as they stumbled together to Terry's truck. Kevin lifted Zipper in, slammed the door, ran around and got in behind the wheel. By now Zipper had shut up. His face was gray. Kevin started the engine and got rolling. He was going for the valley clinic. He reached the main road, turned toward town, and put his foot down.

Driving too fast, you find your mind works better. Kevin didn't think Zipper was going to die, exactly. He didn't think Condosta's dog had had enough of a shot at him to kill him. But Zipper's blood was all over Terry's truck now. He was gray. Maybe he was going to die. Maybe he was already dead.

Kevin pulled into a turn-out, stopped. He took off his shirt and went to work on Zipper, whose hurt side was away from Kevin. Kevin got him turned around and tried to clean him off with the shirt. Blood covered the side of Zipper's head and neck, but its flow seemed mostly to have stopped. Kevin cleaned up what he could. It looked like the dog had taken off Zipper's right ear, the whole thing. That wasn't too bad. Kevin would tell them at the clinic that there had been an accident in the woods, something with a chainsaw. They would believe that. Well, they might believe it. Lucien Silvernail had cut off his ear with a chainsaw.

"How's it look?" Zipper asked.

"Looks like he got your ear," Kevin said.

"My ear? What do you mean? Shit, where is it? What did he do with it?"

"Ate it? Probably he ate it. Sure, he did. Sucker ate it."

"He ate it?"

So what if they didn't believe it they could stick it.

•••••

War. The sad science.

See them there, Kevin and Zipper: huddled, wounded, bleeding, stoic. The stronger, luckier one helping the weaker, trying to pull him through. They might be soldiers. They might be comrades crouched, not in Terry Mackenzie's pickup truck in a turn-out for the town's snowplows, but on the field of honor, having been routed not by Condosta's three-quarter mastiff but by the serried forces of Philip the Fair. And, in either case, set in motion by the same grand historic principle of social boilermaking: feed the young men to the guns.

Feed them to the guns. Before it's too late.

The engine of history, then, at least as revealed in history's undoubted genius for warfare, being the necessity of killing off Kevin and Zipper, thus relieving the pressure their trouble-seeking exerts on the whole social machine. Can it be that we as a nation drown today in our deep criminal soup, not from poverty and the errors of its public relief, not from bastardy, bad schools, divorce—not even from TV—but because we no longer have a good way of letting off the relentless head of trouble accumulated by Kevin and Zipper? Cravenly we are content to have the young men destroy themselves. They will try. They will do their level best. But it may no longer be enough.

•••••

By the time they reached the clinic, Kevin had his story down: Zipper had been in a logging accident. As it turned out nobody asked for his story. Zipper was in shock. They had all they could do to keep him going. They rolled Zipper away on a cart, and Kevin slipped out the side. He drove the truck to Terry's place, left it in Terry's yard.

Condosta's dog was still in the back.

That was the first dog, the one Kevin and Zipper had locked up. They'd forgotten him. Kevin walked home from Terry's. He never thought of the dog. The dog was in the truck all day, all night, and when Terry opened the back the next morning to put in his tools for work, the dog hadn't eaten in twenty-four hours. He came out of there like he was spring-loaded. Terry spoke harshly to Kevin about it later.

•••••

Condosta and the second constable, Homer Patch, stood in the door of the camp. Condosta showed Homer Patch the blood, which looked as though it had been splashed from a bucket over the walls, the floor, the pinball machine, even the ceiling.

"I've seen car crashes with people dead that looked better than this," Homer said. "What happened?"

Condosta was tickled.

"I wasn't here," he said. "So I don't know, but offhand I'd say Godzilla got a piece of him."

"Who?" Homer asked.

"I don't know who," Condosta said. "That's your job."

"What?" Homer asked him.

"I said it's your job to figure out who it was, not mine," said Condosta.

"Oh," said Homer. "No. I mean who's Godzilla?"

"Come with me," Condosta said.

They went around back where Condosta showed Homer the great dog waiting by the corner of the building. Homer was a bigger man than Condosta. He stood over six feet. The head of Condosta's dog was above the level of his belt.

"What do you call that kind of dog?" Homer asked Condosta.

"Bull Mastiff, mostly," Condosta said. "Some Great Dane."

"What's he weigh?"

"Hundred and sixty," Condosta said.

"I believe it," said Homer.

"Gorgo's one seventy-five," Condosta said.

"There's two of them?" Homer asked.

"That's right," Condosta said. "The other's not here. He must be off chasing the breaker somewhere. I don't think that son of a bitch will be out this way again any time soon, do you?"

"You got two of these dogs up here?" Homer asked.

"You got to have two," Condosta said. "They work together. They're trained for it. They work it like a trap."

"A trap," Homer said.

"That's right," Condosta said.

"To tear up some stupid kid who might rip off your plastic boxcars," Homer said.

"How do you know it's some kid?" Condosta asked him.

"How do you know it ain't?" Homer asked.

"I don't," Condosta said. "I don't know. I don't care. They'll take whoever comes. You come in here, they'll take you."

"No, they won't," Homer said.

•••••

Then at last somebody who knew what he was about came down on Condosta's, demolished the door, scooped the cameras, the shortwave, the TV, the weights, the rowing machine, the guns, the power tools, the pinball, the coins, the Lionel cars. Whoever it was didn't waste time trying to figure out how many dogs Condosta had or how to get around them. He shot them both.

Who it was that second time was never known—in contrast to the perpetrators of Kevin and Zipper's fiasco, whom no detective was needed to identify. By the afternoon of the day of their downfall, everybody who cared to know was fully apprised of the reasons for Zipper's being in the hospital, for Kevin's unexpected decision to look for work out of state.

No prosecution was ever started. Nothing had been stolen from Condosta's, after all, and Condosta himself had no backers in town. Besides, Zipper, at least, was generally thought to have had punishment enough. Zipper hadn't been much to look at in the first place, and having an ear bitten off turns out to be a more disfiguring injury than you might imagine. In a small place, the soldiers of trouble have their apologists, they have their protectors.

The final, the decisive factor in the sack of Condosta's was another matter. He remained unknown, unsung, unexplained. Condosta in fact believed he knew who it was who had broken into his place the second time. He believed it was the constable. He felt somehow that he and his dogs and Homer Patch had not hit it off, and that made him suspicious. He had no proof, though, and in the end he dropped the matter. Condosta preferred to be let alone. Anyway, he said, he'd get it all back. He was covered. Like all cops everywhere, Condosta believed in insurance. He was happy, then, except for the Lionel cars. They were gone. For, as Condosta told the others on the first shift at the sunglasses factory in Brattleboro, it's hard to get insurance for such things.

An Incident of the Late Campaign

THE CAPTAIN WENT UP THE STAIRS to the top of his house before seven in the morning. June: the day arriving like a birth, quick, resistless, and wet; the early light slants through the curtained air between the houses, between the old trees, in the momentary summer.

The Captain's house had a tower at the corner that gave it another half-story above the second floor—a useless thing: empty, damp, and cold. They kept it shut up. The Captain went to the tower not long past first light and locked the door behind him. The tower was a hexagon with windows all around. Daylight filled it but daylight was all. The room inside was bare: no table, no chair, no object forgotten from the life of the house below; nothing but the broad pine floorboards, plaster walls, and overhead the complicated framing of the tower's roof. The Captain sat on the floor.

•••••

The Vermont cavalryman must be told to mount his horse, they used to say. An ignorant plowboy, his instinct is to walk behind it. They used to say. However that may be, certainly in '61 we made no great show in the way of cavalry recruits, scarcely knew what to do with them. Therefore Lawyer Burlingame from Brattleboro, young Pease, three others from the Valley towns, and I went over to Albany to enlist. A fine, high, large day in June with everything blowing and growing first rate. It was on such a day we started.

At Albany we made up at the old Rensselaer House, elected as our colonel a man from Schenectady, Lawyer Burlingame his second. But the Schenectady man fell off his horse drunk and broke his neck, and Burlingame was hit at Winchester and badly broke down. So it came to me.

•••••

At eight Abigail came into the kitchen and started a kettle of water on the stove. She hung up her sweater and went to the Captain's bedroom, on the first floor back of the stairs. He wasn't there. She didn't call. She looked for him in the other rooms on the first floor, then went to the door to the cellar stairs. She opened the door, turned on the light, and went halfway down the steps. There she leaned over and looked across the cellar: dirt and junk, dirt and junk. She went back up the cellar stairs, turned off the light, and shut the door.

Abigail went up to the second floor and looked in the rooms there. She found the door to the tower stairs standing open. She looked at it, went to it and looked up the stairs. She drew the door closed. She went back downstairs and into the Captain's room. She looked into the little cabinet where he kept his whiskey. She opened the top drawer of the Captain's desk, looked, shut it. She opened the other drawers, shut them. Then she went back up to the second floor, to the door that led to the tower stairs. She knocked and waited, but no answer came. Abigail opened the door. She was going to go up to the tower, but then she didn't. She closed the door and went back down to the kitchen. There she got on the telephone and called Arthur Ward. Ward lived on the next street, at the end of the village.

•••••

We were chasing Stuart that summer. We were always chasing somebody. We were always moving, always in a hurry. Armies hurrying down out of the hills, flanking each other, rushing, swirling, and spinning together like partners in a reel, like bloody water rushing to the drains of the abattoir Antietam. Twenty-three thousand killed, wounded, or missing on the morning and afternoon of one summer day. Five thousand dead. We never did catch Stuart. Stuart caught us.

•••••

When Ward came up the walk to the Captain's house he found Abigail waiting for him on the front porch. Ward went up the steps onto the porch.

"He was drinking all day yesterday," Abigail said.

"Alright," Ward said.

"I think he's got his gun up there," Abigail said.

"What makes you think so?" Ward asked her.

"It's not in his room," Abigail said. "It's not where it belongs."

"Alright," Ward said.

"Oh, and," Abigail said.

"What?"

"The water," Abigail said.

"Water?"

"Water's going to boil away," Abigail said. "The kettle. I just this minute thought. I put the kettle on when I came, and then I couldn't find him. It's still on. I just this minute thought."

"Can't you go and turn it off?" Ward asked her.

"I'm not going back in there," Abigail said.

"For God's sake," Ward said. He went past her into the house, past the stairs and into the kitchen. The kettle was boiling hard, rattling and hissing. Ward turned it off. Then there was no sound in the house except for the ticking of the Captain's big clock on the kitchen wall. Ward went back out on the porch. The others had come.

There were five volunteer firefighters, the fire chief, and a paramedic. Ward took the chief into the house. No one had told of a fire, but the chief was wearing his big fire helmet and a long shiny yellow slicker. He took the helmet off when they went inside and set it down on the bottom of the stairs.

"Well?" the chief said.

"Upstairs," Ward said. "He might have taken a gun with him."

"Jesus Christ," the chief said. "Has he shot himself?"

"Not yet," Ward said. "He's up in the attic."

"Jesus Christ," the chief said. "Have you seen him?"

"No," Ward said.

"How do you know he hasn't shot himself, then?" the chief asked.

"I would have heard it," Ward said. "I live right by."

"That's right," the chief said. "We best go on up. It's what, half past eight? Everybody's late for work, as it is."

Ward and the chief went up to the second floor. Ward opened the door to the tower stairs and called the Captain's name, but nobody answered. He went up the steps to the door of the tower room. There were seven narrow steps. They were dark, but there was daylight around the door at the top of the steps. The chief followed Ward.

Ward knocked on the door to the tower room. Then he took the handle and tried to open the door.

"George?" Ward said.

"I hear you," the Captain said from the other side of the door.

"What is this, George?" Ward asked.

"You know what," the Captain said through the door.

"Alright, why?" Ward asked.

"You know why," the Captain said. Ward looked around at the chief on the step below him.

"Have you got a weapon in there, George?" Ward asked.

The Captain didn't answer.

"Look, George," Ward said after a minute. "There are six or eight men here. It's Monday morning. They'd like to get to work."

"Let them go," said the Captain. "Let them do what they want. I didn't ask them to come."

"Why not come on down, and they can go, and we'll talk?" said Ward.

"No," the Captain said.

The chief spoke behind Ward.

"Captain Dana, this is Clint Hoover," he said. "You wouldn't have anything to drink in there, would you? I'm about dry." The chief winked at Ward.

The Captain didn't answer.

"Come on down and let's all have a drink, Captain," said the chief. "What do you say?"

"No," the Captain said through the door.

"Listen," the chief said. "Would you rather we came in? Would you rather we busted your god damned door and came in and took you right now?"

"If I were you," the Captain said. "I wouldn't try to do that."

"This is getting no place," the chief said to Ward. He stamped back down the steps out of the tower and down the staircase to the front door, grabbing up his helmet off the last step and booming out the open door.

•••••

Lieutenant Pease it was who found the barn, at sundown four days out: a fine, long barn of the Pennsylvania kind, stone-built below. I proposed to stop there, the barn being hard by the road. Since Friday we had raced Stuart and the men were very much broke down, they could not do more. It had set in to rain. I judged Stuart would put up, too, he must be as tired as we. I didn't know Stuart then.

The men dismounted, led their horses in. Pease saw to the pickets. Two men were required to roll closed the great doors: a fine, long, Pennsylvania barn, a Dutch barn, it may be. The time came later when we would have burned it. Not far to the south, Sheridan burned every house and every barn, burned the crops, wasted over a fine country once so rich. But that time was not yet.

•••••

Ward sat in the dark on the step before the door to the tower room. He heard the Captain, beyond the door, say, "A hundred thousand."

"What, George?" Ward asked.

"A hundred thousand," the Captain said.

"A hundred thousand what, George?" Ward asked.

"A hundred thousand they offered me," the Captain said.

"Who did, George?" Ward asked him.

"Not for the house," the Captain said. "For nothing. For air. *It's not worth that,* I said. *It is to us,* they said. *This place?* I said. *It will cost you that to fix it up. No, it won't,* they said."

"You lost me, George," Ward said. "Who was it said that?"

"*What do you mean?*" I asked. *We're going to take it to the landfill,* they said. Can you beat it? A hundred thousand, and they'd take my house to the dump?"

"Who would, George?" Ward asked.

"You can sell dear and you can sell cheap," the Captain said, "but you can't not sell. Well, not me. Don't mistake: I'd sell it. I would sell it, I expect to sell it. I'd sell it for half that, for less. But I won't sell it so they can take it to the dump. Waste. I won't waste it. *Look,* they said. *You might as well."*

"George, what are you talking about?" Ward asked.

"You know what," the Captain said. "They said, *We can go the long way, too, if you make us. Takes a little longer, is all, costs a little more.*

We don't care. It isn't our money. It's other people's money. It's nobody's money. Eminent domain. We'll put the street right through your parlor, put the electric right through your bed. Water lines, storm drains—hell, gas. Whatever they've got. Then we'll take the place to the landfill. Make it easy, make it hard. We can pay, and we can wait."

"George, that was thirty years ago," Ward said.

•••••

Past midnight Stuart evidently drove our pickets from the east and south; for we heard shots and cries, although none of the guard came in. Presently shot and ball commenced to come through the walls of the barn. The men took cover in the stalls, but there was no cover for the horses. One was soon hit. It screamed and reared, but it was hit again, its leg buckled, and it fell thrashing and kicking, its breath came like a broken bellows, its iron hoofs beat against the boards. Pease shot it at last. A second horse, a fine, big gray, was hit, this one horribly, the ball ripped its belly so that while it plunged and bawled its bowels and lights spilled out, gray and blue, and hung beneath it. As in every war since war was new, the sufferings of the poor great beasts were felt keener, if possible, and are remembered with more pain, than those of wounded men. The gray pitched over but soon got up: its guts drug in the dirt and chaff on the rough board floor. Pease shot it. The stink of blood from the hit horses was as heavy as cigar smoke in the confined air. Stuart evidently proposed to shoot us like rats in a barrel, but that is damned poor sport and wasteful of ammunition. Presently the firing stopped. It lacked two hours to dawn.

•••••

"George, I'm coming in there," Ward said. "I'm going to go down and find another key, and I'm going to come back up here and open the door and come in there."

"If you do that," the Captain said. "I will shoot you."

•••••

The chief came out the front door of the Captain's house and down to the walk. He was a big man, and he took big steps. His long yellow slicker flapped behind him.

"Bring that ladder around here," he called to one of the men. "We can't play around with this fool all day."

"What's the matter with him?" the paramedic asked.

"Drunk or crazy," the chief said. "Throw it right up there, go on," he called. The men laid the long ladder up the side of the tower.

"Drunk or crazy—both, most like," the chief told the medic. Doesn't matter. I'm not playing around with him any more."

"I'm going to try and find Homer," the medic said. He started toward his car.

"No need of Homer," the chief said. "Go on up and get that window open, there. Break it, if you have to. Go on. Go on up there," he said to one of the men who held the ladder.

"Go on up, yourself," the man said.

"Jesus Christ," the chief said. He took the sides of his helmet in both hands and settled it down level on his head, then went quickly up the ladder, his weight bouncing its rails as he climbed. At the top, twenty-five feet above the ground, he looked in at the tower window. The morning sun was on it, and for a moment he couldn't see inside. The chief held up his arm to shade the window and reached for the sash with his other hand. He looked into the tower again. A white room, bare floor, plaster walls, water stained, and what?

The Captain, looking straight at him, sitting with his back against the wall, the opposite wall, bracing a what? A revolver. An ancient revolver a foot and a half long with a barrel that looked as big as a water pipe, bracing the thing on his raised knees and looking at the chief, aiming, his face twisted at the other end, the only safe end, of that long barrel. The Captain cocking the revolver, the muzzle coming up like a tunnel and...what?

•••••

Seventeen men and fifteen horses. Stuart might open on the barn again with the chance of hitting some of us and the certainty of further reducing our mounts, or he might wait til daylight and fire the barn. I judged he'd fire the barn. He was in a hurry. The butcher's ball was to open that very day or the next at latest, and Stuart must be there. He was a dancing man. Five thousand killed.

•••••

Ward, on the step outside the door of the tower room, jumped up and began banging on the door.

"George, my God, what was that?" he cried.

"Your friend tried to come in the window," the Captain said inside the room.

"Hoover? My God, what happened?"

"I told him," the Captain said. "He was warned."

"George, what have you done?" Ward asked.

•••••

Homer Patch was helping on a chimney job in North Ambrose, but he always told them at the store where he was likely to be, so the paramedic was able to reach him. Homer listened on the phone at the house where they were working.

"We just got started here," Homer said. "We were up on the roof."

"I'd come right ahead, if you can," the medic said.

"Well, let me get cleaned up," Homer said.

•••••

The chief sat in the grass at the foot of the ladder and looked up at the tower. His lap and the grass around him were full of pieces of glass, wood, and paint. The chief's helmet was gone. Blood was coming fast from a cut on his head and dripping off his chin into the grass. He sat in the grass like a child and looked up at the broken window in the tower. The medic was with him. The medic held a bandage to the chief's head.

"I'm hit," the chief said. "The son of a bitch has shot me."

"I don't think so," the medic said.

"God damn it, I'm hit," the chief said.

"See if you can get up," the medic said.

The chief stood up. The pieces of glass, paint, and wood fell from his lap into the grass.

"You're okay," the medic said.

"I'm okay," said the chief.

"See if you can make it over there," the medic said. He had the chief around the waist and tried to move him toward the cars and trucks of the firefighters, parked in the street in front of the Captain's house. The chief knocked his arm away.

"Let me be," the chief said.

•••••

Seventeen men and fifteen horses.

Near dawn one of Stuart's lieutenants hailed us from outside. He informed us that our pickets were shot or captured and the barn invested. The lieutenant then desired us to execute a battlefield surrender to himself, whereupon we might retire on parole to Harper's Ferry, retaining our mounts and all equipment. Otherwise Stuart proposed to fire the barn. A young man, the lieutenant seemed to be, and fancy spoken in the old-fashioned way so many of them had. The rebel officers took themselves for gentlemen. We whipped them in the end because we had fewer illusions.

I thanked him. I declined. I mounted the men, and we waited in the barn for first light, the horses nerved up, stamping, restless, though the men had drug the two dead animals to the rear of the building and covered them with hay. We were sixteen men mounted, two double. I proposed at first light to break out and make a gallop for it, dividing the men, to join at a crossroads we had passed the day before, five or six miles west. Any that reached there by seven would form and ride on to the big fight making up around Sharpsburg.

Lieutenant Pease had no mount. Him I told off to open the barn doors on my order. He would remain behind and take his chance. Young Harrison Pease was the only man in our company from my town, indeed, by then the only Vermont man left beside myself. I left him because he was my second and because an officer in command cannot be seen to favor.

"Lieutenant," I told him, "I will see you up home. When this is over, I will buy you a drink, up home."

Pease waited at the doors. He believed he could roll them alone. We others sat our mounts close before him, formed in threes, the horses blowing and stamping in the dark. Then dawn was in the window. There came a shout from outside, and firing, and a rattle above, along the shingles, as their firepots landed on the roof of the barn. A man appeared at the window, outside. I threw my sidearm down on him and fired, the window burst out, and the man disappeared. Pease flung himself on the great door, and our company broke out whooping. The roof was already afire.

•••••

Homer stopped his car down the street from the Captain's house. In front of him was a truck with the door open and the chief sitting in the front seat on the passenger's side, drinking a cup of coffee. He had taken off his coat. Around his head, a clean white bandage with a red spot the size of a half-dollar.

"What happened to you?" Homer asked the chief.

"Bounced, mostly," the chief said. "I came down the ladder in one step, I guess. Jarred some. Cut my head."

"You're lucky," Homer said.

"He's lucky," said the chief. "Not me. Him. This town has been tiptoeing around him for twenty years. He's crazy, he always has been. He ought to be in the bin. Now maybe somebody will put him there."

"I'll talk to him," Homer said.

"That's what I mean," the chief said. "Jesus Christ."

"Is Arthur here?" Homer asked.

"Inside."

'"Why don't you tell everybody to go home?" Homer asked.

"Look," said the chief. "There is a lunatic at large here. He is armed and dangerous. He has about blown the head off a town officer. He has threatened to shoot anybody who tries to take him. You want to send everybody home. What do you need, Homer? Anyplace else, they would have had a sharpshooter on the roof of the next house and this thing would have been over two hours ago."

"You watch too much TV," Homer said. "It's over now. I'd tell them to go home."

The chief watched Homer walk from the street to the Captain's house. Then he dumped his coffee on the ground beside the truck, closed the door, and moved over behind the wheel. The chief gave his horn a short beep and started the engine. At the house the men were bringing the ladder down from the tower.

•••••

Stuart was killed by a stray bullet before Richmond two years later. As far as I know, I never set eyes on the man. Pease I never saw again. None of the men I knew from up home came back, not one. Only me, without a scratch but much broke down and troubled in my thoughts and in the end disgraced. I saw, we all saw, what no man ought to see: the soil turned to mud on a dry summer day, yes, soaked and turned to mire, not by rain but by blood.

Well, they called us to our duty and we went. We all went to it so eagerly, stuck by it so stoutly. Then when it was over and some of us came home, all we found was ghosts. We couldn't tell why, as home was no different from what it had been when we'd left. The houses, farms, the country, the animals, the people were the same. They were not ghosts. They were material. But still something was not right, never right, never to be right. At last we saw it was ourselves. The ghosts were ourselves. We had died as sure as those we buried in Virginia.

And so I say to the young men: don't do it. When they call you to your duty—and they will—don't go.

•••••

Homer went into the Captain's house. Ward was sitting in the front hall where he could look up to the floor above and see the door to the tower stairs.

"Are you going up?" Ward asked Homer.

"Yes," said Homer. "What does he want?"

"I don't know for sure," Ward said.

"Well," Homer said, "why don't you go on home?"

"You go ahead up," Ward said. "I'll wait. I don't like to leave."

Homer climbed the stairs to the second floor and opened the door to the tower steps. He went up. He stopped below the closed door at the top of the steps. He didn't knock.

"You there?" Homer asked.

"Yes," said the Captain.

"Can you get the door?" Homer asked.

The Captain opened the door and stepped aside for Homer, who went past him into the tower room. The Captain shut the door and sat back down on the floor. Homer stood.

"You still drunk?" Homer asked the Captain.

"No," the Captain said. "I'm not drinking today. There's a drink downstairs. You want it?"

"No," Homer said. He crossed the tower room and stood leaning against the casing of the broken window.

"Go ahead," the Captain said. "Go ahead down and fix yourself one. Bring it back up here. I'll wait for you."

"Thanks just the same," Homer said.

"Don't like it any more?" the Captain said. "You used to."

"I do still," Homer said. "I like it all. But I'm working. I'm working now."

"You used to like it, I guess you did," the Captain said. "Do you remember up at camp that time with Junior and those girls from the bus? Hot times. That little blonde? That black girl?"

"I do," Homer said.

"What was it Junior said?" the Captain asked.

"Ice cream," Homer said. "He said, *Look there, boys, we've got ourselves a sundae.*"

"That's right," the Captain said. "That's right. Do you remember?"

"I remember," Homer said. "What happened here?"

The Captain looked at the broken window.

"What happened?" he said. "I don't know. It broke."

"The chief says you took a shot at him," Homer said.

"Who?" the Captain asked.

"Hoover, at the fire house," Homer said. "The new chief."

"Don't know him," said the Captain. "Shot, you say?"

"No," Homer said. "He's allright."

"He fell off his ladder," the Captain said.

"He climbed up it first," Homer said. "He didn't know what he'd find up here."

'No," the Captain said.

"He didn't know," Homer said. "He came to help you."

"Yes," the Captain said. "I know he did."

"Are you going to let me have your pistol, there?" Homer asked him.

"Why?" the Captain asked.

"I'd feel better," Homer said.

"Take it," the Captain said.

He picked the revolver up by its barrel from where it lay beside him on the floor. He extended his arm toward Homer, who leaned forward and took the revolver from the Captain's hand. He turned it, looked at it, laid it carefully on the sill of the broken window beside him.

"I'm surprised it fired," Homer said.

"Did it fire?" the Captain asked.

"They say," Homer said.

"Then I expect it fired," the Captain said.

"It's an old one, isn't it?" Homer asked. "Where did you find it?"

"I didn't," the Captain said. "It's in the family. It belonged to my grandfather. He had it in the Civil War."

"Oh, yes," Homer said.

"He was a cavalryman," the Captain said. "That's a cavalryman's sidearm. He fought right through the war, came back when it was over. It was him built this tower, had it built. He died up here. This room. He came up here and he died."

"Is that right?" Homer asked.

"He lived to a good old age, though," the Captain said. "I remember him, some. I was only a kid. He sat in the parlor. He was a big old man, sitting in there with a blanket around his legs. A big yellow mustache he had, and a kind of loud laugh. A hard laugh. A bad laugh. A laugh like nothing was funny. I remember I was afraid of his laugh. I was afraid of him."

Homer nodded.

"My mother," the Captain said, "didn't like him. Her father-in-law. She thought he was dirty. So he was. She was glad when he died.

That smelly old man, she said once to me. *That evil-smelling old man is gone.*"

"Yes," Homer said.

The Captain smiled. He shook his head.

"Junior," he said. "How he liked it, didn't he? Take on anything that would hold still. What was it he told those girls? What was it he told them it was, monks, was it, up there? A place for monks, out in the woods like that, and didn't they want to come and see the monks? Cistercians, an order of Cistercians, up there, he told them. Poor Cistercian brothers. And we drove them out past Dead River and up the mountain and then we have to walk in to the camp, and the blonde says, *Wow, they really live remote. I'm glad I'm not a monk.* And Junior's got his hand on her bottom the whole way in there and he says, *Me, too.* And then we get there, and he's got that, what was that we had?"

"Irish whiskey," Homer said.

"Irish whiskey," the Captain said. "You slept in a tree, that night."

"I did," Homer said.

"I'm tired," the Captain said. He leaned his head back against the wall and shut his eyes.

"How did he die?" Homer asked him.

"Who?" the Captain asked.

"The old man," Homer said. "The old man from the Civil War."

"I don't know," the Captain said.

"Killed himself," Homer said. "Shot himself. Up here. Right here."

"No," the Captain said. "No, not that. He wasn't that kind. Too tough. Though I don't suppose he was in his right mind."

"No," Homer said. "I don't suppose he would have been."

The Captain opened his eyes. He looked up at Homer.

"Passed that much on, anyhow, didn't he?" the Captain asked.

Homer looked at him. He smiled.

"I wouldn't know," Homer said.

The Captain shook his head again.

"You know, I'm thinking," he said. "When did it all go wrong? I'm thinking about that. When, exactly, was it that the good part ended and it all began to go bad?"

"It, what?" Homer asked.

"You know what," the Captain said. "The selling of everything. The no-value of everything. The waste of everything. The taking it to the dump. What if it was long ago, that it started? What if the good part ended a lot longer ago than we ever thought? What if it started to go wrong long before your time, or mine, what if it was a hundred years ago, more?"

"What if it was?" Homer asked.

"Well," the Captain said. "That would mean we don't remember what we think we remember, wouldn't it? That would mean we don't know what we think we know. Wouldn't it?"

"No," Homer said. "It wouldn't. What do we think we know? Not a lot, not if we're smart. You make too much out of it."

"Do I?" the Captain asked.

"Yes," Homer said. "Look: You remember what you remember. You don't ask for a lot out of it. Those girls that time? That black girl? I thought she was the best thing I'd ever seen. I still do. The night I spent in the tree, there. The Irish whiskey. I don't suppose I've drunk a drop since. That stuff costs money."

The Captain smiled.

"I'm a rich man," he said. "I'll buy you a case."

Say Something?

NOT DULL, THE LITTLE BOY'S EYE, not stupid, not vacant: indifferent. A month short of three years old, he had Homer's, his father's, bland blue eyes, but Quentin's were narrow somehow, somehow unfriendly (but not dull, not slow), almost as if from superiority rather than its opposite. Almost, it was an aristocracy of eye that separated Quentin, that marked him, an altitude, a barrier invisible, insuperable, like high birth. In three years less a month he had not been heard to speak, or cry, or make any other sound. He scarcely moved.

They were riding in Homer's old truck to Caroline's. Friday morning. Caroline was to watch Quentin. Angie was going to her girlfriend's. She said. Homer thought he knew better. He would leave Quentin at Caroline's. Then he knew where to look. They might be at Hugh's, but Homer didn't think so. Hugh was living at home just then, and his mom, who put up with a good deal from Hugh, was an upright woman; she wouldn't put up with that. No, they are roughing it today, Angie and Hugh. They're doing an outdoor thing, a fresh-air job where pine needles get in your underwear, a picnic—or not exactly, but close to.

•••••

Bummer's bus, shot full of bullet holes, sat on its axles among the weeds and brush of its clearing in the woods, smelling faintly of rot, faintly of urine. For twenty years, boys of the town and passing hunters had casually taken it under fire with rocks, slingshots, BB guns, .22s, shotguns, revolvers, deer rifles, even an M16, so that today Bummer's bus looked like the tin cracker box in which your kid (your kid, but not everybody's) has clumsily punched holes so his toad, snake, caterpillar, cat-mauled mouse, winged sparrow won't suffocate.

Angie and Hugh were inside the bus, out of sight below the shotout windows. They might be playing pinochle in there, sitting on old Bummer's rotten mattresses, but Homer doubted it. Angie didn't much care for cards. Homer crouched under the windows of the bus and pressed his ear to its side where the body was pierced by a bullet hole. A moment before, he had heard them talking in there, but then they'd shut up.

"Say something." Homer kept his ear to the hole. It was a big one: you could put the end of your little finger into it. About a .44.

•••••

"What girlfriend?" Caroline said. She kept a playpen set up in her front room for Quentin, and now she knelt beside it, reaching over the rail to smooth Quentin's blond hair. "Which one?" she asked Homer.

"Which one?"

"Which one?" Caroline asked. "She's supposed to be with her girlfriend.

Uh-huh. Okay. Which girlfriend?

"I don't know if she said. Suzanne? I guess Suzanne. What difference does it make?"

"I don't guess any, if it's true," Caroline said. "You know it isn't."

"Look," Homer said. "I asked you to watch him for an hour. You said allright. Are you going to?"

"You know what she's doing," Caroline said.

"Are you going to watch him, or not?"

Caroline stood beside the playpen. She picked Quentin up with some effort and held him in her arms. Caroline was seven years older than Homer, her little brother. She was unmarried (Who would put up with her?), six feet tall. Owned a tongue like a butcher's cleaver. She jogged Quentin, who rode in her arms, a large doll.

"Sure, I'll watch him," Caroline said. She gave Quentin a kiss. "He's got more on the ball than most around here, don't you, sweetheart? Not that that's saying a lot. Look what I've got."

It was Caroline's hope that she could get Quentin to perk up by trying out on him new toys, games, pictures, books, or other objects. Today she had a box full of five or six rubber dinosaurs, each one about the size of a small frog, green, prodigiously horned, spiked, toothed.

"I never heard of a kid who didn't care for dinosaurs," Caroline said. She put Quentin back in the playpen and began to set the dinosaurs out on the floor before him.

"I appreciate it," Homer said.

"You're going where?" Caroline asked him.

"Uh, just over to the mills," Homer said. "Mancuso over there has his truck for sale."

"Mancuso, huh?" Caroline said.

"That's right."

"Uh-huh," Caroline said. "Uh-huh. Well, I've got a hair appointment for noon."

"I'll be back before then," Homer said. "I don't need an hour."

"She doesn't, anyway," Caroline said. "Need an hour. Ten minutes, fifteen's plenty. You know what I mean."

•••••

An outdoor thing, a fresh-air job, a picnic out at Bummer's old place, a kind of sacred grove: green, quiet, dense with the memories of ancient misbehavior.

Somebody driving by had seen the bonfire, heard the music and the whooping. Got home and called right up to complain. Why? Whatever hell the highschoolers were raising out there, they were a mile from the nearest house. Nobody had to listen to them, nobody had to be bothered by them who didn't want to be. The complainer didn't care. Somewhere, somebody was having fun. It had to stop.

Valentine felt the same way. He took a baseball bat with him on calls like this one, and if some kid full of beer gave him a reason to swing it, he was well pleased. So Valentine and Homer drove out to Bummer's old place on a spring midnight. Ten years ago? More like fifteen.

When they could see through the woods the fire and the figures around it, Valentine left Homer and went out to the right so as to come in the other side of the clearing and drive the high schoolers like game to Homer. Homer was to wait for them in the woods, but instead, as soon as Valentine was well away, he went ahead in.

Twenty high schoolers, a third of them pretty much passed out, the rest standing in a kind of daze around the fire, holding beers. No music now; the radios must have run out of battery. So had most of the revelers. One girl knelt at the edge of the woods being helped to throw up. That's the kind of party they always are. Homer walked into the firelight.

"Shit," said a boy when he saw Homer.

"Time to go home," Homer said. He didn't know the boy. Most of the others he did. Hugh hadn't been there that night, or if he had Homer hadn't seen him.

"Come on," Homer said. "Val's coming around the other way. You know Val. He'll have to check everybody out, call everybody's home. He'll make it hard. Go on, now."

"Fuck him," said the unknown boy. "Fuck him and fuck you,too."

Valentine was going to love him.

"No," a girl said then. "He's right. He's being good. Let's go." To Homer she said, "Thank you."

That was Angie. Angela Browning. Homer knew who she was, more or less. There was no lack of Brownings: six or seven kids. Father worked sometimes, sometimes didn't. Mother? Something about her, but Homer didn't know. He knew some of the other kids. He had been in school with some of Angela's much older brothers. She was, probably, a junior that fall. She had long hair then. She had been wearing some boy's jacket, but Homer couldn't tell whether she was at the bonfire with a boy. She might have been with the one Homer didn't know. Come to it, the way things got to be, that would be about what you'd expect.

"Thank you," said Angela Browning. And she and most of the others straggled off into the woods toward the road.

A few minutes later Valentine arrived from the far side of the clearing.

"Where did they all go?" Valentine asked Homer.

"I don't know," Homer said. "Most of them must have got away."

"Sure, they did," Valentine said. "Because you let them. Honest to God, I don't know about you."

Valentine and Homer put out the fire, roused the passed-out kids, cleared a few out of the bus, sent them on their way. By the time they were done it was near three.

"If you're just going to let them go like that," Valentine said, "I don't know why we come up here in the first place."

"Neither do I," said Homer. But he did. He knew then, and thenceforth. He knew, and after that he started breaking up the high schoolers' bonfires pretty regularly, at least for the two more years until she graduated.

•••••

Homer had waited for them. He had lain on his stomach under ferns at the edge of the clearing. Bummer's bus was forty feet from his place, in the middle of the opening spotted with black fire rings. Halfway around the edge of the opening from where Homer lay, a path led out to the road. If Angie and Hugh were coming, they'd come from there.

He heard them. A car stopped. You couldn't see the road. He heard a car door slam, then a second. From where they had left Hugh's car to the clearing must have been a hundred feet. Homer expected he'd hear them on the path, but he didn't. He didn't hear them, and then the dog was there.

A big dog, a black retriever with a red bandana around its neck for a collar, came out of the woods, crossed to the bus, circled it, then started back toward the path to meet Angie and Hugh, who now came out of the woods together.

Homer had forgotten about the dog. It belonged to Hugh. Homer got right down in the ferns. The dog hadn't found him, but what if it did? What if he had to deal with the dog? What if he had to wrestle the dog down to keep it quiet? What if it came about that Hugh was rolling around inside the bus with Homer's young wife while out in the brush Homer rolled around with Hugh's young dog? They would be into something then. Homer might have brought his gun with him. He was second constable, wasn't he? He kept a gun. He might have shot the goddamned dog, then, if it interfered with him. Hugh was in no position right now to object, was he? Still, you couldn't tell what he would do if his dog was shot. Hugh was trouble, he went right ahead, and he and the dog were always together. Homer wondered if the dog got a crack at Angie too.

Angie and Hugh, Hugh's dog following them, approached the bus. They weren't talking, they weren't touching. Angie walked a little ahead. At the door of the bus they didn't wait. Angie went up first, climbing the steps into the bus ahead of Hugh, as though she had business with him there, as though she was showing the place to Hugh to sell it to him. Who does own that bus? Homer had never thought of Bummer's bus being somebody's property, but doesn't everything there is have to belong to someone?

Even Bummer, who had brought the bus there, hadn't been known to own it. The bus itself was an old yellow school bus put out to grass from a western city. Bummer, origin and last name unknown, a 300-pound waif maned like Wild Bill Hickock and bearded like Odin, had brought it to a stop in front of Clifford's store one summer day in, about, 1970. Told immediately and in no uncertain terms to move on, he announced that it was impossible: the bus had died.

They hitched the thing to two tractors and hauled it a couple of miles out of town to the top of Back Diamond Mountain. Their idea was to get the bus rolling down the mountain and see if it wouldn't start. They did. It didn't. At the bottom of the long hill, they gave up. They stopped the bus, hitched it up again, and pulled it another mile to where a logging track came out to the road. They dragged it up the track into the woods to where the log landing had been. There they unhitched the bus, and there it stayed.

Bummer lived in it. He had the bus fitted out as a kind of junk-yard seraglio: rear seats taken from cars for couches, a hammock, curtains on the windows, rugs on the floor, scented candles, red and blue lights—and mattresses, eight or ten of them, covering the whole after end of the interior. Out in front, on the hood, Bummer or somebody had painted in red an enormous star, in fact, the fell pentagram, unholy symbol of the mystic union of flesh and spirit. (Symbol too, or pretty close, Homer thought, looking at it from his hiding place, of Texaco.)

In the bus Bummer lived out the summer like an evil Thoreau, a stoned Thoreau holding out in the woods a party that had no beginning and no end, run on God knows what outrageous chemicals, entertaining every idle and unsavory character in parts of three states. In the fall Bummer put a stove in the bus, stuck the pipe out one of the windows. But even Bummer didn't have a supply of whatever kind of juice it takes to do the winter they have up there in a defunct school bus. By Christmas he was gone and was seen no more.

Since then the bus had fallen or settled into the ground some. The wheels were gone, and the windows and sides had been shot up, but the bus had endured as a ruin, a place where the piping young of the district repaired to fool away their lives, like ignorant shepherds who frolic in the shade of broken monuments, antiquities they are too rude to understand.

•••••

So, yes, Homer had known her. Sure, he had. The way Caroline put it, where Angie was concerned his eyes were open as well as his pants. What did he expect, then? He knew what she was. But what was it he had known she was? Younger, a lot, but more than that. Wild, is what Caroline said Angie was. She wasn't. Angie was not wild but she was something like it: stubborn. She was as tough as Caroline, that maybe being why they didn't get along. But Angie hadn't Caroline's tart certainty. She didn't have as much fun out of her will as Caroline had out of hers. She was like a person who is determined to get what she wants but hasn't and won't because what she wants is to take back her life, take it right back, and you can't do it, nobody can—and she knows that, too. Sad. And then there was Quentin.

Finished school, Angie worked at a farmstand summers. Winters she waitressed. She moved in with her boyfriend, Hugh. Hugh was working, too, some of the time. They lived together in an upstairs bedroom that Mrs. Tavistock rented out of her house at the end of the village.

•••••

Homer had watched the bus for some minutes after Angie and Hugh went in. No sign inside of them. Well, they'd be lying down. No sign of the dog. Still he had waited. Did he expect the bus would begin to shudder, to rock? Nothing was to be found out with him hiding in the woods. He'd have to close in. He couldn't safely look into the bus, but he could listen. He stood and walked gingerly, quietly, out of the ferns and across the opening. He came to the side of the bus opposite the door. There he knelt with his hand on the metal side and put his ear to the bullet hole.

"What are you doing?" Angie said.

"Nothing," Hugh said.

"Is that nothing? You're not. No, cut it out."

Homer, listening outside, let his eyes slip over the portion of the clearing beyond the bus, over the woods, up to the sky, blue and bright, where changing clouds streamed past the steep, sharp edge of the roofline. *Say something.*

"What are you doing later?"

"Going home."

"I'm going by the Wheel tonight."

"Good for you."

"Meet me there."

"How am I going to do that?"

"Just do it."

"What do I tell him?"

"Tell him you're going out. Tell him you're going out with me. You think he cares?"

"No, I mean Quentin. What do I do with him? Bring him along? Buy him a beer?"

"Give him to Cal. She likes him, I thought."

"He's there now."

"Well?"

"No."

"Alright, yes, take him. Just take him, and go."

"Sure. To the Wheel, right. That'd be fun."

"No, I mean for good. Just go."

"Go where?"

"Anywhere. Get out."

"With you? Go with you?"

"Yes. With me."

"Seems to me we tried that."

•••••

No, Angie wasn't wild, but Hugh was. Hugh was trouble in those days. They had fights. Not arguments or disagreements, either, but the kind of fights the guy almost always wins.

One night Mrs. Tavistock, whose house they lived in, called Homer because Angie and Hugh were going at it so badly she was scared. Homer went over there alone. There was a steep wooden stairway built onto the side of the house. He went up the stairs to their apartment and found Angie had locked herself in the bathroom. Hugh was trying to kick in the door. He calmed down when he saw Homer. He sat on their bed. Homer told Angie to come out of the bathroom. When she did he saw Hugh had given her a bad lump over her eye. Homer turned to Hugh. Hugh got to his feet. He started for the door, but Homer caught him before he reached it, picked him up like a bale of hay, and threw him out the second story window. Angie was crying on their bed.

"Can I do anything for you?" Homer asked her. Angie shook her head.

"Can I get anybody for you?" Homer asked. "Do you need to see a doctor?"

"I'm fine," Angie said. "Get out, okay? Just get out, now?"

"I'm trying to help you," Homer said. "I'm trying to see you'll be okay, here."

"I know," Angie said. "But you got him out, didn't you? You already helped. You helped a lot."

"I mean more than that," Homer said.

Angie dried her eyes.

"What more?" she asked.

•••••

Homer took his ear from the side of Bummer's bus and looked around. Hugh's black dog was standing behind him. When Homer turned, the dog sat down on its haunches, put its head on one side, and looked at Homer out of that dog's face at the same time human, familiar, sympathetic—and not getting it, not ever: perfectly wild, perfectly remote.

"Say something," Homer whispered to the dog.

The dog wagged its stiff tail once, panted. Homer got to his feet, watching to see what the dog would do. The dog did nothing. Homer began to move away from the bus back toward the woods. I'm glad that's a flop-eared dog, he thought. They'll give you a break. If it was a sharp-eared dog we'd be into something here. A shepherd, or one of them. We'd be right into something, then.

Inside the bus Angie said, "Cut that out."

"What's the matter?"

"I don't like that."

"You said you did."

"I lied."

•••••

She lied.

"Well, sometimes you have to lie," Angie said. "You wish I hadn't?" Valentine finally had him on the carpet, and for no mere matter of going too easy on the high schoolers. Somebody had broken into Condosta's place off the Bible Hill road. They had broken down his door and cleaned the place out. Condosta's toys—the cameras, the short-wave, the TV, the weights, the rowing machine, the guns, the power tools, the pinball machine, the coins, the Lionel cars—all gone.

Condosta thought Homer had done it. Homer had been to Condosta's to investigate an earlier attempt at a break-in. He'd seen the place. He knew of the valuables Condosta kept. Someone had seen Homer's truck or one like it parked along the road near Condosta's on the night the theft occurred. Condosta had been a cop himself and so distrusted all cops. He accused Homer and got Valentine to believe him.

Valentine had an office in the firehouse. He had Homer hauled up in there. Valentine was explaining to Homer the charges that were going to be brought against him unless he could prove he was somewhere else when Condosta's was broken into. Homer had best get a lawyer, Valentine was telling him, when Angie came into the office.

"Something I can do for you?" Valentine asked Angie.

"You can let my boyfriend go," Angie said.

"Your who?"

"You heard me," Angie said. "He couldn't have gone up there Tuesday night."

"Why not?" Valentine asked her.

"Because he was with me," Angie said. "He was with me then."

"The whole night?"

"The whole night," said Angie.

So Angie and Homer were in a way married before they met, like Oriental royalty, they were joined before they converged, by means of a lie, and not a regular lie but a lie that Homer, and Angie, and anybody else who cared knew to be a lie. A lie that was meant not to deceive but to reveal, the first one such but not the last. And out of them had somehow come this poor, strange kid who couldn't or wouldn't talk, wouldn't even look around him or take notice, who seemed half doll, half fish, half lord. Where in the world had they got him from?

•••••

Caroline was sitting with a cup of coffee in her front room watching Quentin, who sat in the playpen with his new dinosaurs arranged in a circle before him. He might have moved since Homer had left them an hour ago, or he might not have. You couldn't tell.

"That was pretty quick," Caroline said.

"Sure," Homer said. "I'd been here ten minutes ago but I stopped by Suzanne's. She was at Suzanne's, like she said. They like to watch that show, what is it?"

"Uh-huh," said Caroline. "Get you some coffee?"

"No," Homer said. "Is he ready?'

"Why wouldn't he be ready?" Caroline said. "He's ready."

She lifted Quentin out of the pen.

"He's getting some weight," Caroline said.

"He is," Homer said.

"Going to be a big kid," Caroline said. "Like you were."

"Yes," Homer said. "Well, she was at Suzanne's after all."

"She was, huh?" Caroline said.

"Yes," Homer said. "She says hi."

"Hi to her," Caroline said.

•••••

"Sometimes you have to lie," said Angie after they had left Valentine's office.

"You wish I hadn't?

"No," Homer said. "But why did you?"

"Well," said Angie, "you helped me. More than once. You always tried to help. I mean to help you."

"It's my job," Homer said. "Helping you, I was doing my job."

"Oh, I see," Angie said. "That's all it was, was it? Doing your job?"

"No," Homer said.

"You wanted more than that," Angie said. "You said you did, didn't you?"

"Yes," Homer said, "I did."

"You did?" asked Angie.

"I did," Homer said. "I do."

"Well, then," said Angie.

•••••

Quentin was asleep in his little room upstairs. Did he sleep? Anyway, he was up there. Angie sat on the edge of their bed in her nightgown with her back to Homer. She was brushing her hair. Homer lay in the bed and watched her. He watched the faint freckles that were scattered across her shoulders move with her skin when she brought her arm back to brush her hair.

"I saw Hugh," Angie said.

"Hugh?" Homer said.

"He said he's been looking for you," Angie said. "He's missing his dog. That black dog he has?"

"I know the one."

"He's missing him, he said. He said if you see him."

"I'll look out for him." Homer said. "Where was it you saw Hugh?"

"At Suzanne's," Angie said.

"He was at Suzanne's this morning?"

"Yeah," Angie said. "He was."

"Well," Homer said. "Well, his dog's okay."

Nobody knew why Quentin didn't talk. As far as anybody could tell he had the equipment for it, for anything he needed. Oh, you could go to doctors who had names for the kind of kid Quentin was, but the names didn't tell you anything. They dwindled away like a brook in summer. The names came to this: he didn't talk because he didn't talk. You could leave him behind all day long, you could take him to Caroline's, but at night when you got home, there he was.

Homer lay on his back in the dark. Angela slept, or anyway she lay quite still, her bare shoulder turned up, white, undefended. Sometimes Homer had a dream, or, not a dream, but the kind of idea that passes by before you sleep, an idea about Quentin, connected with that old New England story about the kid who never speaks. It seems this kid, a farm kid in the old days, never says a word. He gets older, gets big, now he's seventeen, eighteen. Never a word out of him, like Quentin. His parents have long since decided he's damaged, dumb, mute. Then one day the mute kid and his father are crossing a field and the bull spots them and charges. The father doesn't see it coming but the kid does, and he yells, "Look out, Pa!" So they both run like hell, get over the fence just ahead of the bull. And they're lying there panting and puffing and the father looks over at his speechless kid and says, "Thought you couldn't talk." And the kid says, "Didn't have nothing to say till now."

Say something, Quentin. Say something, now.

"Tell him his dog's okay," Homer said in the dark. "Tell him I'll help him find his dog."

The Sister's Tale

WHOSE KID WAS IT A YEAR OR SO AGO over here to the Four Corners, along there someplace, that had a hole in his heart, like, some kind of abnormality, born with it, and it looked as though he'd had to have it fixed or it would kill him?—just a kid and had to have some godawful kind of operation, it seems like somebody said it was thirty, forty thousand dollars it was going to cost, so no way did they have that kind of money and the people up here set about to raise it for them? That's right, they put on raffles and sales and whatnot, and went around and asked, five dollars, ten dollars, twenty, and in five or six weeks they had it, most of it, maybe twenty-six, twenty-seven thousand, all raised right here. Pretty good. Well, it was.

Silvernail. It was Silvernail's kid. And Clay Makepeace over here on the way to North Ambrose made up the balance, eight thousand dollars I believe it was. Well, he just wrote them out a check, you see, he won't miss it, and so the kid had his operation and now he's okay. Remy Silvernail. I believe he's okay now. He's working in the woods with his father. So must be it was more than a year or two ago, it might have been five or six. A hole in his heart it was he had, like a hole.

Well, yes, I thought that was pretty good, how everybody helped them, but then my little brother said,

"Well, it was just money."

"What do you mean?"

"People don't really help each other out the way they did," he said. "They don't neighbor together the way they used to."

"Oh, they don't?"

"No," he said, "they don't. Neighbors don't help each other. Instead of neighbors now we've got the social service worker, I guess, or somebody like that, and when people do help at all, they don't work, they just give money, like here what you have been talking about."

"You really believe that?" I asked him.

"I don't know," he said. "Yes, I do. Sure."

"You do?" I said. "Where was it you grew up? Somewhere around here, was it? Or am I wrong?"

"Oh, boy," he said. "Oh, boy. Alright, same place as you."

"That's what I thought, too," I said, "but are you sure? It seems as though you are remembering someplace else. You know as well as I do what a lot of that neighboring you think so much of was, and you know what it wasn't."

"What do you mean?"

"It wasn't all helping, was it?"

"I don't know what you're talking about," my brother said, but I said to him, "Yes you do."

•••••

I was the only girl. It was a whole bunch of men and boys, and me. Our father always took me when he could when there was work to do, because I was as strong and as big as any of the boys, and, he said, and Cal's not a fool, either, Father said, she's not a damned fool the way a boy is. I must have been sixteen or seventeen, so my brother was ten or eleven. He went too. Our father took us to help get Mr. Holiday's wood in for him. Holiday was one of the old-time farmers then, and he was past working, so a bunch of people turned out in the fall to help him get his wood in. Help him, is what they said. Do it for him, is what it was.

There must have been twenty-five or thirty came. Most of them were up in Holiday's woods. They would get logs out of the woods and down to the bottom of the hill and then we'd go over and put a chain on them and draw them to the yard to get cut up and chopped and into Holiday's shed. We lived nearest and Father and we two kids had driven over on the tractor he had then that he called the Iron Horse. My brother still has it, still runs it.

At Holiday's nobody was going into the house. They had a big fire going down in the yard and if you got cold you went over there to warm up, but you stayed clear of the house. Nobody wanted to go into the house if they could help it. Holiday was in there and he'd just as soon bite you.

So our father and me and my brother would ride over to the log landing, and my brother and me would take the chain and bend it onto a log and our father would be sitting up on the tractor and he'd crank the log up behind, you see, so it would pull, and then he'd take it up and pull it away. We two would follow along walking. That was the way we worked it, like that, back and forth from the log landing.

Then on one trip we were going back to the yard with a log and he was up ahead on the tractor and I remember I was watching him when it was like the tractor kind of jumped forward, *oops*, and Father stopped it and turned around on the seat real quick, just whipped around, there, and looked back where we were to see if we were okay.

The chain had broke. We didn't hear it, didn't see it snap back, like, the way they can, which was why he'd turned right around when he felt the log slack off.

That's why we had to go up to the house, because Holiday might have a bolt Father could use to patch the chain together. My brother didn't want to go and I didn't either, but our father didn't ask us. He just said, you know, *Come on.*

I don't know who has that place now, that house. It stood empty for a number of years after Holiday's time. He was one of the real old-time scratch farmers up there, about the last of them, even then. Never had electric, never had running water. When he started, I guess that whole hill was little places like that, a half-dozen cows, but even in my time they were all gone except Holiday's and he wasn't up to much for farming even when he was strong and by this time he'd given up working the place at all, hadn't animals any more, he'd about let everything go down. After Holiday died it stood empty, then it seems like somebody bought it. Now, I don't know. I don't suppose I've been out that way for ten or twelve years. It's funny how you don't get around.

We went up to the house. It was a slum. Well, it was. The yard full of old iron and junk. I don't truthfully know how Holiday got by, you know? How did he live? I don't truthfully know. Today he'd be in a home of some kind, well that's where he ended up as it was. The house, it seemed like half the windows were out. Holiday lived in the kitchen, just dirt, dirty.

Well, we'd hardly walked in the door than he started on us. I'll never forget it, him sitting in that filthy kitchen, and I mean filthy, not disorderly but filthy, sitting in a busted out stuffed chair with his bad leg stuck out on some kind of cracker box and just lighting into us before we'd hardly walked in the door. *Where have you been?*, like. *I ain't got a stick of wood here, not a stick, I ain't had for a month. Do you know how cold it gets here mornings?* It was cold in there, too, cold and evil smelling like Holiday sometimes, you know, used the corner which I have no doubt he did. *What have you been doing? I been waiting here a month for you. I ain't got a stick of wood and I been waiting here all by myself, I liked to froze.* Like that. Gratitude, you know? It's a beautiful thing.

Father knew how to take him, though. He paid no attention. That was his way in things: get on with it and don't waste time figuring out who's wrong. So he just went over to where Holiday sat and said hello, asked him how he was. *Terrible,* he said, Holiday said, *terrible,* and then he started in on all his infirmities, like: can't walk, can't stand up straight, can't raise this arm above here, all day he can't piss—that's how he said it—all day long he can't piss and all night long he can't stop pissing. That accounted for the smell. Holiday had a bed, more of a cot, set up right there behind the kitchen stove, all twisted-up greasy blankets, it looked like an animal's bed. He was carrying on about his aches and pains, and then Father asked him did he have a bolt, two-incher, and he shut up and thought, just shut right up. *Might, at that,* Holiday said.

Then he tried to get up from his chair but he couldn't so he asked, ordered, more like, our father to hand him his stick, which Father did and Holiday got up and stumped over to a corner of the kitchen and started picking through a tin box full of junk he kept over there and pretty soon he came up with a bolt and handed it to Father and then he started in going through another box he had and he found a nut and two washers to go on the bolt and handed them over. And he asked Father why he needed a bolt and Father told him his log chain had broke and then Holiday started in on us again worse than before. He'd been okay for as long as he was finding the bolt and whatnot but now he just took off, only worse than before, like, *Next time you see to it you bring a sound chain not some trash or you fix your own goddamn chain,* you know, and then: *It ain't bad enough I got to sit here and freeze for a month while you dub around, but then when you do come I got to fix your equipment for you.*

Well, I lost it.

I did. I lost it. I was never much for holding my tongue, if I got something to say I say it. I won't say I've never wished I'd shut up, but that's not my way, it seems like. Well, I said, to him, Listen to me: there are twenty-five people out there who have better things to do who have come the whole way out here to do your work for you and you have got no right to talk like you do, you're nothing but a charity case and if it weren't for them you'd have to go into a home of some kind, so you can just shut up.

Well, that stopped him. He looked at me it might have been for the first time, and *Who's that?* he asked Father. *Who's that?*

So Father said that's my daughter Caroline and Holiday said to me, *What are you talking about, I don't go into no kind of home. I don't go noplace. They come to me. They have got to come. You think they come for nothing? They have got to. I ain't going to be around forever, you know.*

He went back over to his chair and sat and picked up his bad leg in his two hands and dropped it on the box with a thump. He was hot. Then Father said we'd best get back to it and we got ready to go, but Mr. Holiday was looking at my brother. He hadn't opened his mouth.

That your boy? Holiday asked Father. Yes, Father said, this is Homer.

Holiday looked hard at my brother for a minute and then he said, Come here, like, *Here, come here, come on over here,* looking at him.

Homer didn't want to. He was scared of Holiday. I could tell he was, but *Go ahead,* Father said, and he took about two steps toward Holiday and Holiday said, *No, come right up here* and Father kind of nudged him and said, *Go ahead, now.*

So my brother had to come up beside his chair, close. Then Holiday kind of squirmed around in his chair and dug into his trousers pocket and he took something out and showed it to my brother but I couldn't see what it was. *You know what this is?* Holiday asked him, and I heard my brother say Yes. *You want it?* Holiday said, and my brother said something like, I guess so. So Holiday passed the thing to him and as he did it he kind of looked around my brother, where he stood by his chair, to my father and me, and he put the thing in my brother's hand and closed his hand over it. *Here, you take it,* Holiday said. *You keep it, it's yours. Hang onto it. Don't ever lose it. Don't ever give it away. Most of all, don't let her have it. Don't even tell her what it is.* Saying, like, *HER. Don't tell HER. You do, it won't be no manner of good to you.*

Don't tell *HER,* you see. Looking at me.

Tell him thank you, our father said, and my brother said it. Then we were going, Father gave Holiday a cigarette and lit it for him and we left him there in his chair, smoking. When we got outside and our father had gone on ahead, I asked my brother what it was Holiday had given him and he said, *Nothing, a dime, nothing.*

Let me see, I said, and he said *No,* but I got him by the wrist and made him open his hand and show me what Holiday had given him, and that's all it was: a dime. Like it was some big secret thing when all it was a dirty dime.

•••••

Understand that this happened a good many years ago and I don't remember now how far along in the day we had been when the chain parted or how long we worked after it got fixed, but we went back to drawing logs down to the yard and then it being November along of four in the afternoon it began to get dark so the party broke up. The wood we had cut that day filled Holiday's shed and there was a lot more stacked between the shed and the house, three or four long, straight stacks of new wood, it makes a pretty sight. Well, it does.

About everybody had gone and me and my brother had climbed up on the back of the tractor behind our father and were getting ready to start home, and we were in the yard facing the house and the lane and the door opens and here comes Holiday stumping along on his stick. He kind of stands there in the dooryard and looks around and he sees his shed full of wood and the new stacks all handy. He is right in front of us, you see, and he looks at the woodpile. Well, he doesn't say a word, walks right over there and no kidding he walks up to the nearest stack and he looks over at us and then he undoes his trousers and like pulls himself out, looking right at us the whole time, and he commences to, you know, urinate on that woodpile. Just like that, doesn't say a word.

Well, my little brother began to hoot and the other boys who hadn't yet left began to hoot, and Father yelled at him, *Goddamn it, Amos, put that thing back where it belongs there's ladies,* you know, but he's hooting too and pretty soon Holiday finishes up and arranges himself, like, and then he takes an armload of wood off the stack and proceeds back into the house. We started the tractor and went home, my brother was carrying on like he'd been to a show and Father didn't say anything but he thought it was pretty good too.

•••••

That filthy, ignorant old man, you know? And now of course today my little brother says, "What do you mean? Holiday never did anything to you. There wasn't any harm in him. He was just one of those old fellows, he hadn't long to live."

"Oh, really," I said. "Is that what he was? Is that what he was to you? Of course, it wasn't you he showed himself to."

"What do you mean?" he says. "He didn't show himself to you, either. The man was taking a leak."

"Oh, is that what he was doing? I wasn't sure."

That's right, and here this little town, where the people complain they can't afford another ten bucks on their taxes so the school can have a clean well, and it's true a lot of them can't, these people raise, they freely give, the best part of thirty thousand dollars so that Silvernail kid can have his lesion fixed, his heart lesion. And so when my brother says, *Oh, it ain't the same, people don't help each other out, people don't neighbor together the way they did, it seems like it's all money nowadays,* I'm obliged to remind him that that famous neighboring of his wasn't always exactly what it looked like—and anyway, I tell him, stacking cordwood is one thing, stacking wood, that's something you know how to do, I tell my brother, but if it was a hole in my heart and you my neighbor, well I guess I'd just as soon take the money.

Charity Suffers Long

As soon as Makepeace shut the door of his truck he knew he didn't want to go around and look in the back, and in that instant—a second, less than a second—there leapt up before him the whole damnable affair complete, its stupidity, its pain, its threat to his precarious rehabilitation: the missing saw, the ratlike kid, the down tailgate, Homer Patch and his whore of a wife and their poor, unfinished boy (named?...named?). The entire business reared up in his path like a horrid weed, root, stalk, and flower—doubt, insult, memory.

Of course the saw was gone. The truck bed lay gaping, as empty as the midnight coffin of a sojourning vampire. Had he forgotten to put up the tailgate? Had it popped open on a bump, pitching his saw out into the road? Had the rat-kid, having ripped off his saw, let the tailgate down precisely so no one could know for sure that the saw hadn't fallen off the truck? Had he that kind of subtlety?

Makepeace sat on the tailgate. In a minute Monica, who had heard him drive up but hadn't seen him in the house, came out into the yard.

"What is it?" Monica asked.

"Saw's gone."

"Who's gone?" Monica asked. She stood by the truck.

"My saw," Makepeace said. "I picked it up at Alva's. Put it in the back, drove home. Now it's gone."

"It fell off."

"I don't think so," Makepeace said. "What's the name of those people in the trailers, there before you come into the Mills? I picked one of them up. He was hitching near Alva's, so I picked him up. He got in back, rode in back. When we got to the trailers he banged on the cab and I pulled over and he got down and I saw him. I bet he took it."

"Benware," Monica said.

"That's right. What's the name of the skinny one with all the tattoos? Kind of like a rat?"

"I know who you mean," Monica said. "I don't know his name."

"I bet he took it," Makepeace said. "I practically gave it to him, didn't I, the way he'd look at it?"

"Wait," Monica said. "Zipper."

"Zipper?" Makepeace said.

"Zipper Benware," Monica said. "You mean Zipper, I think."

"Zipper. How in the world do you know him?"

"His sister does hair," Monica said. "You know her. The heavy girl."

"They're all heavy," Makepeace said.

"If you think he robbed you, call the police," Monica said.

"What police?"

"The constable," Monica said. "Call Homer Patch."

"Jesus," Makepeace said. "Not Homer."

"Why not?"

"He's no good," Makepeace said. "Besides, there'd be no point. They're all in it together, aren't they? It'd be like calling Jesse James to catch Frank James."

"That's simple nonsense, Honey," Monica said.

"Is it?"

"You know it is," Monica said. "Homer Patch is a nice guy."

"Did I say he wasn't?"

"I always think of that poor kid."

"What's he got to do with it?"

"Nothing," Monica said. "He has nothing to do with it."

"Not Homer," Makepeace said.

"Well, okay," Monica said, "Then you'd best just leave it. Forget it. Get a new saw. It won't break you."

"You can't call him," Makepeace said. "He's never home."

"He doesn't want to be home," Monica said.

Makepeace sat on the back of the truck and shook his head. Monica, standing, leaned toward him and laid her hands on his thighs. She put her face up to his and kissed him. "Honey?" she said. "Keep it for the important things, okay, Honey?"

"Right," Makepeace said. He smiled. Monica released him.

"Well," she said. "Look: you don't know that he took it. You don't know anybody took it. Maybe it did fall off. Why don't you drive back down toward the shop and look for it along the way?"

Makepeace looked at her. "I could do that," he said.

He doesn't want to be home.

•••••

"Okay. Move."

Zipper pulled Makepeace's saw from the brush beside the road and trotted up the drive toward his trailer. Nobody was around. The dogs started barking, but they knocked off when they saw Zipper. His trailer was built up two feet to keep it out of the mud and the dirt and the dog shit, and the steps were wrecked. Zipper threw open the door, tossed the saw inside, and climbed in after it. He shut the door. In a second he was back out with the saw in a feed sack rigged with a sling so he could hang it on his back while he rode. Time. Zipper figured he had an hour and a half, no more, less if the man reached Patch. Call it an hour. One thing: he couldn't be here. Move. Zipper slung the saw behind him and straddled his bike.

Halfway across the yard, Zipper gave it some wrist so he'd be going too fast and watched Kevin's junker sitting beside the other trailer on his right. Kevin's piece of crap Walker dog was there, and as he went by the dog came out from under the car and went for his flank, but Zipper took his right boot off the peg, swerved in, and gave the dog a shot in the chops that made him sing, having behind it all Zipper's hundred and nineteen plus whatever he picked up from the moving bike. The dog rolled twice, and before he recovered and got back in the ring, Zipper was out of there.

•••••

If the rat-boy didn't take the saw, then presumably it was still on the truck when he got off—unless it fell off before the kid appeared, which was unlikely as he was hitching not more than fifty feet from Alva's. Therefore if the saw fell off the truck at all (as opposed to its being removed by the rat-boy), it probably did so between the trailers, where the kid got off, and home. So if it's going to turn up beside the road it will be pretty near.

Gronnnk.

Makepeace, dawdling along looking for his saw beside the road, was nearly rammed in the rear by a big truck that had come up close. He pulled off the blacktop and the truck went around him with a roar, a delivery truck that rode high and swayed on its springs. SARATOGA the rear doors said. Jesus.

Here Lies
CLAYTON MAKEPEACE
Adopted son of old Vermont
While he was looking to change his luck
He was
BUGGERED
by a high-priced water truck
Memento Mori

Not Homer.

Why not?

They're all in it together. The rat-boy is probably Homer's cousin, his nephew, his grandson. Homer and the rat-boy's old man probably supped from the same bowl, swung from the same birch. Before the white man came.

Simple nonsense, Honey.

Is it?

Makepeace drove gingerly back onto the road, first looking carefully behind him. It had come to pass in his own hard, wild country, America's first frontier, where seven generations of lonely hill farmers had died in despair and been buried in little graveyards not less rocky than their impoverished pastures, that today a man could be killed by a truck carrying fizzwater to the lotus-eaters pleasuring amongst the resorts under Stratton Mountain. Fizzwater. They didn't even drink gin anymore, the way lotus-eaters ought to do.

Up ahead, three boys tagging along in the dust, empty-handed.

"Seen a chainsaw lying in the road anywhere along here?"

"No."

"You know what a chainsaw is?"

"Uh-huh."

"It's yellow."

"Uh-huh."

"If you find it, could you turn it in to Alva's shop?"

"Uh-huh."

"There's a reward."

"Uh-huh."

You never got anything out of their kids. He didn't, anyway. Some did. You had to admire, say, teachers, social service workers. Even just parents: they have to talk to kids sometimes. Or possibly not. Homer's son, now. (His name? The boy's name? I know it. Reginald. Not Reginald. I'll think of it.) Profoundly damaged. Not damaged, some such phrase. I'll think of it. Defective. Not defective, but like that. Middle-aged memory an instrument of torture: you reach for the fruit of memory and it vanishes, to appear when you no longer want it. Not defective, but that idea. Doesn't speak and nobody can speak to him. Profoundly damaged. But, then, look at those three there, and they're presumably a hundred percent. Not a large gap here, you could say, between the lucky ones and the others. So, as in the famous Calvin Coolidge story: how can they tell?

Homer's a nice guy.

He is. Steady. Not too much in the brains department, maybe. I know him, oh, forty years. Homer was in the old hay crews. He was always part of haying. I used to come up to help, and one time we were working at Johnson's and we'd finished work after dark, and Homer and I wound up talking. "Homer's getting married," Johnson had said earlier. "I don't know, I thought he had more sense." So I said to Homer, you know, Good luck, and I asked him when was the wedding.

"September," Homer said. I asked him if he and his girl expected to stay in town.

"They'll have to," Johnson said. "They'll have to stay in town. The bride ain't been weaned yet."

It seemed Homer was getting ready to marry a girl not long out of high school, ten or twelve years younger than he. Johnson and the hay crew thought it was a great joke. They wouldn't leave it alone.

"Come the big night," Johnson said. "Old Homer gets her in bed, he won't know whether to you-know her or burp her."

Homer laughed with the rest of them.

"Tell us, Clay," Johnson said to me. "You're studying law. If the girl marries an adult does she get to vote right off?"

Homer turned to me. "Yes," he said, "we're staying here. We might as well. There isn't anyplace else."

The thing is, I don't want to call him.

Why not?

I'm not sure.

Homer directing traffic at the fall fair. Homer tearing rotten clapboards off the side of somebody's house, a bright pile of new ones waiting at his feet. Homer up on people's roofs in the hot sun; somewhere he'd learned to hang slate. Homer picking up a case of beer at Clifford's. Homer driving out to the house the time Monica hit a deer with her car not killing it; taking a rifle out of the back seat of his constable car. Homer running with the others to put out a brush fire. Homer driving around the town, waiting alongside the roads. Homer helping to search the woods for madmen, suicides, lost hunters, lost children.

I'd like to take care of my own trouble, the way they do, the way he does. I'd like to be the one giving help, not getting it.

Well, Honey, sure you would. Who wouldn't? But right now you aren't. No shame.

No?

•••••

Zipper found Kevin at Fairbrother's log job off the road that goes into the state forest on the far side of Round Mountain. They had quit for lunch. Kevin and Terry Mackenzie were sitting on the bed of the crane truck going through a giant box of Dunkin' Donuts and a half-gallon of Pepsi. Zipper wished Terry would go away.

The skidders had cut the log yard up into ruts so badly that Zipper couldn't get his bike in there. He left it on the road, took the feed sack with Makepeace's saw inside it, and made his way to Kevin and Terry.

"So, Zipper babes," Kevin said.

"How you doing, men?" Zipper asked. Terry Mackenzie just looked at him.

"I've got a piece of equipment here, okay?" Zipper said.

"Is that so?" Kevin said.

"I'm here to make a sale," Zipper said.

"Is that right?" Kevin asked.

Zipper took the saw out of the sack and laid it on the truck bed beside the box of doughnuts. "My, my," said Kevin, but Terry only snickered and shook his head.

"That's a lot of saw for a little guy, Zip," said Kevin.

"It's practically new," Zipper said.

"Practically new, but not, you know, new," Kevin said. "Is it?"

"Not really, no," Zipper said. He'd known he'd have to let Kevin jerk him around some, either way. Terry being there made it worse.

"So what do you figure you need to get for it?" Kevin asked him.

"Two-fifty," Zipper said. "It'd sell for five hundred new, okay?"

"Yeah, it would," Kevin said. "So, uh, where did you say you got this almost new saw, Zip? I bet some rich guy died and left it to you in his will, like, didn't he?"

"Yeah," said Zipper.

Kevin picked up the saw and set it on his knee.

"So what do you think?" he said to Terry Mackenzie.

"Piece of shit," said Terry.

"That's what I think," Kevin said. He tossed Makepeace's saw like a heavy log into Zipper's arms. "You piss me off, Zip," Kevin said. "You think I'm dumb? Get out of here, I'll get Bobby Fairbrother over here and he'll kick you right the fuck off his mountain."

•••••

Makepeace turned in at the garage and small-engine shop, where he'd collected his repaired saw an hour earlier. A kid with no shirt and a lot of chest muscles was putting gas into a jerk-wagon, a black pickup truck the size of a light battleship that sat up on four enormous tires, its axles raised a yard in the air. When Makepeace drove in, the kid put away the hose and motioned for him to pull in to the pumps, but Makepeace shook his head.

"I'm just getting turned around," he told the bare-chested kid, who looked at him and went back to fueling his barge.

Makepeace got back on the road the way he had come. He wasn't going to find his saw beside the road. It wasn't there. Maybe he would call Homer. Go on home now and call him. Or forget it, the way Monica said. Or how about this? Go there. Go to Homer's and see him.

He doesn't want to be home. He probably wouldn't be around. Still, going is better than calling. Why? Going there is better than calling him as if he were a handyman. Why?

That's what he is.

He approached the three boys he'd passed on the way to the shop. They walked beside the road as before, their eyes on the ground, but now they had a prize. The biggest boy carried it along, not Makepeace's saw, but a runover cat dangling by its tail. The boys marched along among the roadside weeds in a file, at the rear the tallest sweeping through the weeds the road-killed cat. A reassuring sight: childhood's antique dispensation. Kids, boys anyway, in every age, even ours: however shamefully we cheat them, neglect them, sell them short, leave them to be content with bad ideas, bad food, bad schools, lies, dope, and advertising, a dead cat will fetch them every time, exactly as it did Tom Sawyer and Huckleberry Finn by the banks of the Mississippi long ago. Homer's boy. (His name? Monica will know.) He'd be, say, twelve. Deficits. Profound deficits. Monica had worked with such kids at one time. She saw it right away.

Profound deficits. Deficits was the word. Not the right word, but straight out of the modern phrasebook: the equivocal, inaccurate poetry of bad news. A deficit can be corrected in time, can't it? Not this one.

Why?

For no reason. Chance. If you run the line a million times, two million, then on the two million and first it's going to screw up. If you're the one waiting at the end of the line for yours when it does, well, tough. Homer's wife. Angie. Angela. Had her tubes tied. Who blamed her? The dice have no memory. They don't know it's you again.

So you didn't want to be home. That was where the boy was. It might not be so hard when he was a baby, especially if he was the first. The families help, the neighbors. But by and by they mostly fall away, like tired runners in a long-distance race. And he gets bigger, and he doesn't. On nice days sometimes he'd sit in a rocking chair on Homer's porch or out in the yard, sit there like something in a store window, dressed by somebody else in new clothes that he outgrew but never wore out. He'd rock back and forth in his chair for hours, hours; the chair might have been on a motor. The boy could walk, but he didn't on his own. He stayed where you parked him, like a car.

You must feel like you can't do it any more, not another day, not another hour. But you've got it to do. And the thing is, almost not him but you. You're getting older. And what then?

•••••

Jake's truck wasn't at the shop, but Zipper rolled in anyway and left his bike by the Coke machine. He unslung the saw and carried it in through one of the bays. Alva was at the big bench in back, running the wheel. Zipper stood where Alva could see him and waited for him to get done. In a minute Alva turned off the wheel and put up his glasses.

"Jake not here?" Zipper asked.

"He's on a job," Alva said. "You want to call it that. We used to call it something else."

"Where is he?"

"Patches'," Alva said. "Angie called."

"Oh," Zipper said.

"Said her car wouldn't start. Jake went out there to jump her." Alva looked at Zipper. "It's a service business, son," he said.

"Yeah. Well, how long will he be?"

"Knowing Angie, not real long," Alva said. "You can wait."

"No," Zipper said. "Look." He took Makepeace's saw out of the sack and set it down on the bench. "I got this from Kevin, okay? Some guy on Fairbrother's job quit and gave it to him because he owed him money. Kevin doesn't want it—okay?—and he asked me to bring it in here and see you about it. He'll take two hundred. You can give it to me and I'll get it back to Kevin." Alva turned the saw on the bench and looked at it. "You're quick," he said.

"It's practically new, okay?" Zipper said. "How do you mean, quick?"

"Well," Alva said. "I just serviced this saw for Clay Makepeace this morning. An hour ago he seemed to think it was his. He paid for it like it was, anyway. Now it's yours. That's quick. Why don't you go on out to Patches'? Jake only just left. Moves like yours, you could probably get in and out of Angie before old Jake remembers what it was he went there to do. Go ahead. Don't forget to take your saw."

•••••

Well, what are you supposed to do? Six years before, seven. Monica knew about a guy at Children's Hospital. A good guy. Not cheap. Makepeace had gone to Boston to Roger Davenport's office and asked Roger to cut a check on his firm so it wouldn't come from Makepeace.

"I'll do it, but it's a mistake," Roger had said.

"Why?" Makepeace asked.

"It's too much money, Clay," Roger said. "I don't mean you shouldn't give it to them. Of course you should. But if you're going to be charitable, be charitable. Go to him. Tell him you'd like to help and give him a check. Don't try to be anonymous. There's nothing but trouble there. For one thing, it won't work."

"It might," Makepeace said.

"There's simply no chance," Roger said. "Look: just give it to him."

"I can't," Makepeace said.

"I don't understand why not."

"I can't."

A week later Angela Patch about ran him down as he came out of Clifford's store. She slammed to a stop nearly on his toes, her old car rocking on soft shocks. Makepeace, though vertical, was not in great shape himself, the hour being past nine in the morning and the period the most missing part of his Dark Ages, an unending Precambrian in which the only objects of knowledge were obscure creatures, alive only by definition, that sat on the bottom of the vast shallow sea that covered everything. He stopped and stood blinking in Clifford's parking lot like an owl taken by noon.

Angela flung the car door open, got out from behind the wheel, and went for him like an angry dog, waving an envelope, the envelope from Christie, Davenport.

"This belongs to you, doesn't it? Doesn't it?"

"It belongs to you,"

"It does like hell. You sent it. You did."

"Yes."

"Well, then, take it," Angela said. She was shouting. She threw the envelope down at Makepeace's feet. "Take it, you fuck. We don't want it. Our boy doesn't want it."

She had always been a plumply pretty girl, but now her face looked as if it had been clamped in a vise. Makepeace didn't move. Angela picked up the envelope and shoved it at his chest.

"Take it. Take your fucking charity."

Everybody in Clifford's had gathered at the door. Then another car pulled up behind Angela's. Homer got out and came around toward them.

"Ange," he said.

"Tell him," Angela shouted. "Tell him to take it." She twisted Makpeace's envelope up in her hand and swung at him. Makepeace stepped back and let her fist go by. Homer got Angela around the waist and picked her up. She kicked.

"Tell him we don't want it," Angela shouted.

"Come on, Ange, he's not giving it to you," Homer said.

He moved her back toward her car, half-carrying her, trying to soothe her, keeping her feet off the ground so she couldn't fight him. Angela was crying. Homer stuck her in her car and drove away, leaving the other car where it was. One of the women who worked at Clifford's went to Angela's car, leaned in, and turned off the motor, then went back into the store. Makepeace stood alone in front of the building with the people who had gathered there looking at him. After a minute most of them went back inside.

So Homer's kid stayed home. Twelve now, more. Was fed, was bathed, was dressed—*Jesus*—was wiped. Getting bigger, stronger. Angela? Angela got up to all kinds of things, Monica heard. If Homer couldn't be found around his house by day or night, it looked like every other able-bodied male in the town over fifteen and under ninety could. The thing is, you didn't want to be home. The thing is, you must come to hate him—do you?—hate your own flesh the way the fox hates the limb that the steel trap holds.

I'll think of his name.

•••••

That's it. Time's up. Dump it. Or get rid of it someplace.

Zipper left Alva's shop and took the road back toward his place. A couple of miles along, where the road ran through the woods, he slowed and pulled his bike over at a place where an old logging track ran into the shadows. He looked up and down the road, then dismounted and rolled his bike a little way into the trees up the track. He left the bike where it couldn't be seen from the road. He took Makepeace's saw in its sack and walked farther into the woods. In a couple of hundred feet, the log track disappeared. Zipper stopped.

Off the track to his right was a pine as wide at the bottom as a barn door. Zipper went to it. At the foot he laid Makepeace's saw in its sack on the ground. He wasn't going to bury it. He was going to cover it with brush to keep it hidden until he came back for it. He went down on his knees and with his hands began raking pine needles and little branches over the bundle.

Zipper looked up. Three kids had come around the tree from the other side. The tree was so big that Zipper hadn't known they were there. The three looked at Zipper as he tried to cover up Makepeace's saw. They were only little kids.

"What are you doing here?" Zipper asked the kids.

"Nothing."

"Nothing? What have you got back there? You're smoking, right?"

"No."

"No? Well, let's just see."

Zipper went around the big tree. On the opposite side the boys had dug out a shallow hole. In the hole lay a black-and-white cat, dead.

"What's this?"

"Nothing."

"What are you doing here, then?"

"Burying him."

"Yeah? Yeah, well, do you know who I am?"

"Uh-huh."

That's it. Not that it would have worked, anyway, probably. Zipper knew he wouldn't have been able to find the place again. His luck didn't run that way. Another guy goes down to the corner for a pack of cigarettes and a Megabucks ticket and next morning he has a hundred million. Zipper goes down to the corner for a pack of cigarettes and a Megabucks ticket and the next morning he has an old Megabucks ticket and the next year he has lung cancer. Luck. Zipper went back around the tree, picked up the sack, and brushed it off. The boys followed him. Best dump it. Zipper turned.

"Look," he said to the boys, "any of you want to buy a saw?"

He left the woods, got on his bike, slung the saw behind him, and headed back the way he had come, past Alva's, through the village, and onto the road that led to Brattleboro. Before he reached the village he passed Homer Patch, sitting in his constable car by the roadside. Homer started his car when Zipper went by him and followed him, not too close. Mile after mile, Homer was back there, and by the time they reached the town line he had Zipper talking to himself.

"That's right: I found it in the road, back there, I was just, uh...So, now you got a law against riding around with a chainsaw, huh? You got a law against just riding around with a chainsaw, I guess."

"We do if it ain't yours."

But then Homer's car slowed and dropped behind, turned around in the road, and started back the way they had come.

That's it. Dump it. Dump the sucker.

•••••

Makepeace drove into Homer's lane and stopped in front of Homer's house. The black jerk-wagon from Alva's was parked beside Homer's little porch, and inside the house a radio was playing, too loud. The bodybuilder kid must be inside, then, with Angela. Makepeace decided to wait for him to leave, then decided not to. He left his truck and went to the house. He had reached the porch before he remembered Homer's boy. Where was he? A kitchen chair stood on the porch, but it was empty. Makepeace crossed the porch and looked through the screen door. He could see into the kitchen through the screen. Nobody was in the kitchen, but the music from the radio was so loud he could feel its base through the boards of the porch. Makepeace had never been inside Homer's house. He knocked on the screen door.

The radio went off, then went on again, but turned down. Makepeace saw through the screen a woman come out of a room off the kitchen and come toward him. Not Angela. She was barefoot and wore a man's T-shirt that hung to her thighs. The T-shirt said HARLEY DAVIDSON. Makepeace saw that the woman was Angela, after all. When had he last seen her close? He had been fooled by her hair, which had been blond and soft and was now red and loosely curly. Angela stood on the other side of the screen door. She did not open it.

"Yes?" Angela said.

"Uh, I'm Clayton Makepeace."

"I know who you are," Angela said. "What do you want?"

"I'm trying to find your husband."

"He's not here."

"Do you know where I can find him?"

"No," said Angela "He's around."

At that moment, coming not from the front of the little house, where Angela had evidently been when Makepeace knocked, but from overhead, an upstairs room, a muffled banging began, a thumping, not rapid but steady, like the drip of water on a slab, a noise as though someone above was stamping one foot, heavily booted, on a bare board floor.

Angela's eyes stayed levelly on Makepeace when the banging began.

"He's around," she said. "I'll tell him you were here."

"Alright," Makepeace said.

Angela stepped back from the screen door and left Makepeace standing on the porch. Just before she disappeared into the front of the house, she turned.

"Go on," she said to Makepeace. "Go on, now. I'll tell him."

Angela was gone. The banging from upstairs went on, not louder, not less loud, until suddenly the radio was returned to top volume, on which the banging stopped. Makepeace left the porch and went to his truck. He started the engine and turned around in Homer's yard beside the elevated jerk-wagon, preposterous, improvident, and cheap. She ran the radio that way not to help bounce her new boyfriend but because she'd found it was a way to shut the other up.

At the end of the lane Makepeace came upon Homer waiting in his constable car. Homer had backed into the woods so he couldn't be seen from the house and so if you were coming out of the lane you wouldn't see him until you were right in front of him. Makepeace stopped. He started to get out of his truck, expecting Homer to come and meet him, but Homer didn't move. He stayed in his car, and so Makepeace didn't go to him. Homer sat there in his car ten feet away, looking at Makepeace.

Not Homer.

Why not?

I'd like to be different from the others.

You think you aren't, Honey?

No. I know I am. That's the thing. So is Homer—only he isn't.

You're a funny man, Honey. I think you need a job.

Something, anyway.

Then Homer waved, a flick of the fingers that rested on the steering wheel of his car. Makepeace waved back. He started his truck and drove out of the lane and off toward his home.

You know. You know what I have been here to do and what not. What are you waiting for? The kid with the silly truck? Why wait for him? It's your house. Let him go out the bedroom window without his pants. It's your house. What are you waiting for?

Listen, I was looking for you.

I know.

Not her.

No.

•••••

Zipper stopped his bike in the middle of the high bridge that goes over the West River north of Brattleboro. He was northbound. He looked back. A truck and a car were coming up. Zipper unslung

Makepeace's saw and laid it beside the railing of the bridge, then knelt and pretended to work on his bike while the traffic went by.

When the truck and the car had gone past and were off the bridge at the other end and Zipper had the bridge momentarily to himself, he stood and took the saw from the feed sack. Standing on the curb of the bridge rail, he held the saw by its bar and swung it down and to his right, pivoting, then swung back, letting it fly, sailing it out into the air. The bright saw, falling, turned in the air, turned, turned, and hit the river a hundred feet below with a tiny white splash.

Zipper had gotten back on his bike, started up, and was underway before he realized that the saw's teeth when he swung it away had cut his right hand and there was blood all over. The sucker got him for sure, and so it looked like saw one, us nothing, but what are you going to do?

•••••

I would help them hay. I didn't belong with them, but I was present, and they let anybody help at haying who wanted to—and how I used to love the work. Two weeks in June, then again several weeks later except in some dry years. In school and then college vacations, at law school, I helped, then later I took time off and came up from New York. Once or twice I came all the way from Washington for haying. At some farms they would have a gang of ten or fifteen. We'd start out first thing and spend all day in the mowings.

Even then, forty years ago, the enterprise was obsolete. Half the old farms had been given up, and the ones that were left had plenty of machinery; nobody really needed all of us. Hay crews of the local youth were Vermont's House of Lords—a grand anachronism. But, hell, the bales did have to get thrown into the wagons, and at the other end they had to get put up in the barn. There were no machines for that.

Homer was always there too, every year. A couple of years older than I and big and strong always: my height, but thirty pounds heavier. Quiet. He'd drive one of the tractors in the morning, and then in the afternoon, when the loaders were beginning to tire out, he'd get down and pitch bales.

Johnson's top piece was the last we did each year. It was in a bowl on Round Mountain behind his place. There was a track that went up there through the woods for the tractors and wagons, but it was rocky and narrow. One year, I'd come up from New York, we didn't finish the top piece until night had come, and Johnson decided not to try to drive the loaded wagons down the mountain in the dark. So we all started to walk back down to the farm. Johnson always had a keg of beer and all you could eat for the hay crews.

"Homer and that little girl are looking to start right to work to get a baby," Johnson said. "Then they'll have two babies in the house."

The others had gone on ahead. I waited in the shorn mowing for a little while. It was still vaguely light in the open, and in the west a kind of last, fading ribbon of yellow lingered between the black hill-tops and the night sky. There isn't anyplace else. I'd be back on the train to the city the next morning. When I got ready to leave the field and start down through the woods, I saw Homer coming back up.

Today, getting old, we are one man, past all division. He is the unfortunate I, I am the unfortunate he. We are each other's obverse: he, having a home, doesn't want to be there; I, having no home, never want to be anyplace else. But at that time I doubt I'd spoken ten words to Homer in my life, our life. When he came out of the woods and across the dark plain of Johnson's mowing, I said,

"You're going the wrong way, aren't you? Did you lose something?"

And Homer said, "You. I didn't see you. Are you going to stay up here all night?"

Quentin. The boy's name is Quentin.

Round Mountain

SEVENTEEN MEN AND NINE WOMEN HAD GATHERED in the road in front of Patches' by eight o'clock: three from the sheriff's department, the whole office except the dispatch; the same from Clifford's, which hadn't opened at all that morning; two from the inn; half the Fire and Rescue; three game wardens; a couple of the road crew; five Boy Scouts; the rest, casuals, including Makepeace, who came alone, and two others whom nobody had ever seen before. Who would they be? Anyway, twenty- six of them, altogether—counting Homer, twenty-seven.

Valentine looked them over. He had run these actions before, more than once. He thanked God for the wardens, and he thanked God for the Scouts. They would go all day. So, maybe, would the deputies. Most of the rest would have dropped off by noon. Though after all, if you didn't find him by noon, were you going to?

Who were those two? Were they together? They didn't seem like it. Hard to say. Often when you called for volunteers on a search party a stranger or two showed up, guests from the inn, people from the campground. Vacationers looking for something to do, wanting to help. Well, let them help. Ringers. When they had gone up Back Diamond Mountain looking for Johnson's crazy aunt, a ringer had shown up, a big tall customer wearing horse-riding pants, for Christ's sake. Never said a word, did everything he was told, stayed with it all day, and turned out to be a United States Senator from Mississippi or Carolina or one of them.

Valentine called them out. Most were still drinking coffee from paper cups that the people from Clifford's had brought. When Valentine spoke up, the ones who hadn't finished their coffee poured out their cups carefully on the road and got ready to move. Going past the house, they set their paper cups down on the front porch.

He led them around behind the house to the brook and across into the trees. The brook here ran close to the base of the wooded hill, Round Mountain. On the flat before the slope began to go up, Valentine stopped them. Homer was with them, he saw. Homer had come out of the house when they'd started, and he was with them now. Valentine thought he might have waited with Angie and Cal, that might have been best. Probably he hadn't wanted to listen to the women go at each other over this thing. Anyway, here he was and who was going to tell him he shouldn't be? He knew what he was doing, he knew the country, and say whatever you want to about it, it was his kid that was missing. Valentine closed them up and began to explain what it was they were going to do.

•••••

Caroline found she didn't want to sit at the table with Angela, so she stood at the kitchen sink and looked out the back window. She watched the search party cross the brook and go into the woods.

"Do you want more coffee?" Angela asked her. "There is more, if you want it."

"If I drink another cup of coffee I'll jump out of my skin," Caroline said.

"I feel like I could sleep," Angela said. "But I know I wouldn't."

"You might try," Caroline said.

Angela shook her head.

"No," she said. "If someone does call, one of the others, I want to take it. That's why he left us here, isn't it? That's why we're here instead of looking."

"Come to that," Caroline said, "I could stay for the phone and you could go. It doesn't need two."

"Well," Angela said, "he said to stay. He knows what he's doing. In something like this, he knows what he's doing."

"I hope so," Caroline said. "Anyway we all act like he does."

"He does," Angela said. "They'll find him."

"Sure, they'll find him," Caroline said. "But not out on the road where somebody will call in here. Nobody's going to call. He's up there and that's where they'll find him."

"If they find him," Angela said.

Caroline turned from the sink and looked at her.

"Yes," she said. "If."

•••••

How They Started

"Alright," Valentine said. He stood before the search party with his back to the hill, where the woods went steeply up from the brook, then seemed to level off.

"Alright," he said. "Who hasn't been on a line search before?" Five or six hands.

"Alright," Valentine said. "Not much to it, really."

He would be the point, a few paces ahead of the rest of them, in the line. He would hold the compass and use it to keep them straight up the hill. They would take positions, say, fifteen feet apart. Each of them was to keep that space between him and those to his left and right, and keep part of an eye on Valentine, so the line advanced in order. Beyond that, they were to go slow and watch the ground ahead of their feet. If anybody found anything, or couldn't keep up, he was to call out and the whole line was to stop.

With twenty-seven, Valentine thought he could stretch them from the powerline much of the way across the hill behind Patches'. He would take them straight west, up to the top of Round Mountain. If they didn't find Quentin, then he'd decide whether to go on down the other side or swing them and return in a second sweep back to the road.

"Keep it slow," he told them. "You aren't in a race. Keep it slow, keep your distance either side, and keep looking. Watch the ground, the ground. This kid don't fly. He's up here. He's been up here all night. He's cold and tired. He won't be moving. He'll be down. Watch logs, brush, holes. He might be unconscious, might not."

Valentine stopped. He looked for the ringers. All the others knew Quentin. The ringers were at the back of the group, listening. One, a man in his forties, fifties, bald, the other younger; both wore shorts. Grown men wearing shorts? They didn't know Quentin, they didn't know about Quentin.

"The thing is," Valentine said. "He's not right in the head. Not simple, but not right. He hears us coming, he won't call out. He don't talk at all. If he hears us, see, he might not know what we are. He might even get down, try to hide. Watch the ground. If you come to a piece you can't cover alone and keep up, stop and sing out."

Homer stood at the back of the group, near the ringers.

"Clothes," Valentine told them. "He might have dropped clothes. Look for them. He was wearing, what?"

"Tan pants," Homer said. "Red shirt. Sneakers."

"Look for them," Valentine said.

The bald ringer spoke up.

"How big a boy is this?" he asked. "I mean, is this a little boy, is this a child?"

"Right," Valentine said. "No. He's big. My size, about. How old?"

"Seventeen in May," Homer said.

"Seventeen," Valentine said. "So, you're not looking for a rabbit. We'll find him. As long as we keep the line and keep looking, we can't not find him. That's how it works. That's a line search."

Valentine and Homer got them stretched out and in place. They were about ready then. In the woods the sun was among the tops of the trees.

"Do you want to point?" Valentine asked Homer. "I can take the end. What do you want to do?"

"I'll take the end," Homer said. "You go ahead."

So Homer went to take up the right, or north, end of the line, the end that anchored on the powerline. The powerline in its rough, broad clearing was on his right. When Valentine saw him in place, he started them out.

•••••

Brave words, Makepeace thought. Keep the line and keep looking and we can't not find him. Unless.

Makepeace had a soft pitch starting out. On his left one of the two he didn't know in the party, the older one, was having to hold on to saplings and the roots of bigger trees and nearly pull himself over a steep stretch. A stocky man, fit, and looking, with his naked dome and his sturdy bare knees below short trousers, like those German tourists you used to see pounding about the Dolomites. Homer, on Makepeace's right, was a little behind, moving into a growth of fern at the edge of the powerline. He poked along with the rest of them, looking, bending to look closer, walking on. How do you do that when it's your own kid? How do you keep it together well enough to tighten down and do the job just as you would for a lost hunter, hiker, birdwatcher? Well, they're trained for it. Oh, indeed? Nonsense. How do you train for that, to search a wilderness for your lost own? Talking about self-control, here. Talking about discipline. Is it good to have that kind of discipline? Should we admire it in you or should we pity it?

Odd that Makepeace didn't know the two newcomers. But was it? In reality, wasn't what was odd that he did know all the others? There must be twenty-five or thirty, and he knew them and he knew a little about them—well, about a few of them. The pretty girl who waited on them at the inn: her name? Kathleen? No. Maureen? No. She had gone off to college, hadn't she, and turned around and come right back? Once he had left her a twenty-dollar tip and Monica had given him a funny look. That was a few years ago. Days of wine and roses. Cindy? Not Cindy. The others, well, not that he knew even that much about them, but he knew them by sight, recognized them—they him, presumably. Sometimes Makepeace believed he was an anthropologist who has lost his ticket home. Who has burned his ticket home.

Brave words. Keep the line and keep looking and you can't not find him—unless he's not here. What then? Then you don't find him. Do you want to find him? Well, of course you do.

Do you?

So dark in here, really, dark and worse: unfriendly, forbidding in a small way. Not like a nice woods where you can walk along and listen to the birds. No birds in here. No real daylight, either, even with the sun up and getting higher. In here the sun made a kind of deep green shade or curtain that parted before you and closed again twenty-five feet ahead, never more. No wonder you needed a crowd to search an area that in open country would barely make a ballfield.

In that country the woods go up the mountain like broad stairs: a level stretch, then a steep one, then level again, then steep. Underfoot the going always difficult, the ground gullied, broken up into hollows and hummocks, any of them big enough to hide Homer's poor boy. What if you don't find him? What if you find him too late? What's worse: finding him too late; not finding him at all?

Or is it this way: finding or not finding him isn't the choice. What, then? Who is it you're looking for up here? I know who we are looking for. Who are you looking for?

•••••

"The thing is," Caroline said, "what can happen to him? Not much. Think about it."

"He's gone all night," Angela said.

"I know that," Caroline said. "I know how long he's gone. So what? Don't you see? Now, if it was any other time of year, I'd worry. Sure, I would. Cold, exposure: sure, you'd worry, then. Not in summer. In summer he's not going to freeze on one night outdoors. Look: people come from all over the country to sleep out in the woods around here in summer. They pay money to do it. Don't they?"

"I guess so," Angela said.

"You know so," Caroline said. "What happened is he wandered around till it got dark, then he crashed. Like he does. He lay down and curled up and went to sleep."

"He didn't go to sleep," said Angela.

"Alright, then, he just lay there," Caroline said. "He's lying there yet. His dad is probably going to trip over him."

"Sure," Angela said.

"Well," said Caroline, "what about that hunter the other year they had to look for? He was out all night in November. It snowed, didn't it? Anyway, it was November, it was cold. They found him. He was okay."

"That's true," Angela said.

"This was going to happen," Caroline said. "It was bound to. You know that."

Angela shook her head. She didn't answer.

•••••

"Hold it," Homer called out. "Hold them up."

He was into a stand of fern growth, waist high, as wide as somebody's living room. He could walk on through it, but he couldn't see the ground. A horse could be lying down in there and you not see it unless you stepped on it. So Homer stopped them and Clay Makepeace, on his left, and the man to Clay's left, who was wearing shorts, a trim little sport with a bald top whom Homer didn't know but took for a tourist, quartered through the ferns while the line waited. They found nothing: no horse, no silent boy frozen in hiding like a fawn. Clay and the other went back to their spots and Valentine got them going again.

Homer kept the powerline clearing off his right shoulder. The powerline lay in full sun now, and the brightness out there and the darkness in the woods made it hard to look from one place to the other and see much. The clearing was grown up in brush, too, some of it as high as your chest. If Quentin was out there and keeping down, you'd never see him, that's true, but a line search has got to begin and end someplace.

Put it this way: if he's where you're looking, you may find him. If he's not, you won't. He'll have to find himself, then.

Mostly, they did. The kid that got lost from the campground last year wandered around all night, finally walked out of the woods in somebody's backyard in Newfane and asked for a glass of water. He'd covered fifteen miles. The hiker everybody was so wound up about because he'd had a bad heart claimed he was never really lost at all. He turned up in the bar at the Wheel, drinking beer.

And then, even when you had to go out after them, you mostly found them if you had any idea at all where to look. The deer hunter missing from Dana's camp had sense enough when he knew he was lost to sit down and wait. They found him not more than a hundred feet from the road. He'd felt like pretty much of a fool for that, but how was he to know? If he'd known where he was, he wouldn't have been lost. Not knowing where you are is what being lost is.

So, Quentin. Was he lost, then? You couldn't find him, but was he lost?

Some you didn't find, or not the way you wanted to. Homer had been reminded of the lost, embarrassed deer hunter twenty different times by twenty different people since yesterday afternoon past four when Angela looked out back and saw Quentin's rocking chair was empty. He had not been reminded of others who had gone missing in the woods. He had not been reminded of Sophronia Johnson, whom they'd found dead on Back Diamond Mountain. He had not been reminded of her nephew, Homer's old boss, who had gone up this same hill, Round Mountain, though on the other side, one day in late fall and never come back. They never had found Johnson. Probably he hadn't wanted them to.

Do you? Do you want to be found? Are we going to find you?

•••••

Not a Prisoner

"What did he say?" Caroline asked Angela. Earlier, she had left the kitchen and gone into the front room. She sat by herself in there on the couch looking at the wallpaper, the furniture, the silent TV. Being in the front room by herself with Angela in the kitchen, also by herself, was worse than being with her. Caroline went back into the kitchen and stood again at the sink. "What did he say?"

"Homer?" Angela said. "You mean to me?"

"Yes," Caroline said. "What did he say, you know, yesterday?"

"I called him," Angela said.

"I know you did," Caroline said. "Did he say anything, you know, when he heard he was gone?"

"No, he didn't," Angela said. "Maybe he said, 'Allright.' What would he say?"

"I don't know," Caroline said.

"He sat out back there by himself every day," Angela said.

"Nobody watched him all the time. Nobody could. He wasn't a prisoner."

"I know," Caroline said.

"I could, you're saying," Angela said. "You're saying I ought to have had an eye on him. What was I doing?"

"No," Caroline said.

"Yes," Angela said. "Sure, you are. You know what? I don't mind. It doesn't matter. He knows that. He didn't say anything because it's not important any more."

"Allright," Caroline said.

"Time was, maybe he would have said something," Angela said. "At one time, maybe, but not now. We're a long way past that now."

"You and him, huh?" Caroline said.

"That's right, us. We are past that. Maybe you aren't. I don't know. We are. We're past that now. We have left that behind."

"Allright," Caroline said.

"He wasn't a prisoner," Angela said. "Homer said: 'This ain't a jail. What's he done wrong to be in jail? He's not a prisoner.' So this happens, and now we have got to go find him. That's all."

"Alright," Caroline said again.

•••••

The sister's name? Not Lorraine, but like that. An old-fashioned name from before they began to get their names from TV. Louise? Not Louise.

Makepeace peered into a tangle of branches head high, the top of a fallen tree. He thrashed at the branches with his stick and broke some of them down so he could see better into the thicket they made. Then he went around it and started on up the hill. On his right Homer had moved out a little ahead. He stopped and waited for Makepeace to come even, then went on.

She had had care of the boy much of the time. Lorna. Not Lorna. A bit of a dragon, really: a hard, plain-spoken piece of goods. She'd have something to say to Mrs. Homer about letting the boy get out here (if he was out here). When she had him, when the sister had him, she watched him with an eye like steel. At one time, Homer had told him, she'd wanted to have a kind of harness made for the boy.

"Cal wants to put him on a leash," Homer said. "Can you beat it?"

"She's worried about him," Makepeace said. "She's worried he'll wander off, hurt himself."

"He's not a prisoner," said Homer. "Anyway he wouldn't get far."

Well, exactly. Talking about control. Talking about protection. What is Cal afraid is going to happen to him? She's afraid he'll wander off. Well, so he has. What of it? Like the man said: how far can he get? Is she afraid he'll get out of the pale, that he'll escape the town's gravity and go slipping off into space? What if he did? What is it out there that they're afraid of? What do they think is beyond their little hills?

Cal wants to put him on a leash. Cal.

Caroline. Her name's Caroline.

•••••

After half an hour Valentine broke them and they rested for ten minutes. Homer left his position on the right and went out of the woods onto the powerline clearing. In the sun the clearing was getting hot. Bees passed over it. Blackberries grew out in the middle of the opening. They grew waist high or more, and they had stickers like a prison fence. You couldn't search them, you couldn't even try. The berries were ripe. Nobody would come out here to pick them. Well, bears. You could find a bear out here but not a boy.

What does a kid like Quentin know? Nobody ever said he was blind, or deaf, or even slow-witted. He didn't look slow-witted. He was seventeen. He had to know something. Did he know when he left the yard? Did he know he'd get lost? Was he lost?

Somewhere around here, Homer believed, was an old place he knew, a cellar hole, several of them. He remembered finding the place once. People had lived up here in the olden days, it seemed. There had been quite a little settlement at the time. He had come on the place during deer season one year—not lately, but some years back. It was up here somewhere: a set of rock-walled square holes not looking big enough to have been houses. Maybe their houses had been smaller in those days. Rock chimney foundation, some busted bricks; ash poles growing up fifteen, twenty feet out of the hole. The bottom full of leaves, old dead leaves. Now, if you got down into a place like that, right down into those leaves, would they ever find you? Not without a dog.

Valentine called him in. They were starting again. Homer went back into the woods, found his spot. The truth was, what Valentine had said about searching mostly wasn't so, that you had to find him. Valentine had said that to keep them keen, but it wasn't true. You didn't necessarily find them. You could fail because of the briars, the holes. Or, for example, if they were looking for Homer and he wanted not to be found, he'd get up in a tree. He would sit up there quietly like an owl and let them pass beneath him in their useless line, a line of moles. They never look up.

Are we going to find you? Maybe we aren't. What then?

•••••

Caroline pulled a chair out from the table where Angela sat. She sat down across the table from Angela, facing her. She put her hand on top of Angela's, on the table.

"Look," Caroline said, "why don't you go on out and look with them? I'll mind the phone. His thing of leaving us both here don't make sense. There's no need. Plus, we'll kill each other if we sit here all day."

"I'll wait," Angela said. "He told me to and I said I would. He knows what he's doing in this better than we do."

"No, he doesn't," Caroline said. "He's just making it up. They all are. Go on and go with them. Go catch up with them."

"They've been gone over an hour," Angela said. "Nearer two. I wouldn't catch them."

"Sure, you would," Caroline said. "They're going slow. They have to."

"I hate it out there, you know?" said Angela. "All the trees, damp, dark. No, thanks. I know how that sounds, but no, thanks. Anyway, I'd never find them. I'd get turned around out there. I'd get lost, too."

Caroline smiled.

"That wouldn't help much, would it?" she said.

"Besides," Angela said. "If somebody does find him somewhere else and calls here, I want to know, you know? I want to know right then. I don't want to have to wait to find out he's found until we all come dragging out of the woods hours from now and don't know anything except that we haven't found him."

"Well," Caroline said, "come to that, here's what we could do. If you went with them and somebody found him and called here, I'd just call the firehouse and get them to start the siren. You can hear the siren all over town. You'd hear it, even up there. You'd know he's found. You'd come back down. As it is, they probably thought of that already, to do that."

"Well, it doesn't matter," Angela said. "I'm staying. You can go catch up with them, if you want."

"I'd never make it," Caroline said. "I'm not young like you."

Angela looked at her.

"I mean really," Caroline said. "I'm not able. Allright, then, we both stay here. We both wait. I just don't want us to kill each other doing it."

"I won't kill you if you won't kill me," Angela said.

•••••

Johnson

On the left, toward the end of the line, they had something. The younger ringer and Ginger, from the inn, had stopped. They were calling Valentine. Valentine held up the line and went over to them. They were pointing into a little gully at their feet, and as Valentine approached, the ringer got down into the gully and lifted out what for a moment Valentine took to be a snake.

The ringer handed it up to Valentine and climbed out of the gully. No snake: a leather belt, broad, black with damp and partly rotten but whole, at one end a square brass buckle. Valentine held it raised so it hung to its full length from his hand. Several of the others had come up. He looked around for Homer.

"This wouldn't be his," Valentine said.

"No," Homer said. "He has a belt but that ain't it."

"No," said Valentine.

The ringer and the girl Ginger had been moving up either side of a little streambed, now dry. The gully, no more than a couple of feet deep, was full of rocks and fallen branches of all sizes that washed down with the water running through it when the snow melted off Round Mountain in the spring. The belt had been hanging over a branch. Valentine held it out to Homer, but Homer only looked at it.

"This has been out here some while," Valentine said. "It doesn't do us any good."

"It's Johnson's," said Homer.

Valentine held the belt higher, looked at it again.

"You think it is?" he asked.

"It is," Homer said.

"Well," Valentine said. "It might be, might not. There's no lack of belts like this."

"See the holes," Homer said.

The belt had six holes made neatly by a leather punch and two more holes, smaller, cut or torn through the leather, maybe by a knife or awl, to make the belt come around tighter.

"He skinnied down," Homer said. "He fixed his belt so it would go on holding his pants up. There wasn't much to him, by the end."

"I guess it might be Johnson's, at that," Valentine said.

Some of them now began looking around, idly, peering down into the streambed and alongside it, poking here and there and kicking up the leaves and trash that made the groundcover in the woods. What were they looking for? Johnson had been gone nine years. If that was his belt they wouldn't even find his bones—buttons, maybe, car keys, nickels and dimes, teeth.

"What are we doing now?" Makepeace asked Valentine. "Who are we looking for now?"

"The boy," Valentine said. He clapped his hands together and gave a shrill whistle.

"Alright," said Valentine. "Hold it up, now. You'll lose the line. Get back to it, now, go ahead. We can't find everything that's lost on this mountain all in one morning."

•••••

What? Wait. Wait, now. Who are you?

Homer stopped. On the far side of the powerline cut a man was walking up the hill, keeping pace with him. He walked at the edge of the woods over there, passing from the glare of the open cutting into the shadow of the trees and out again. He was hard to see: a man not a woman; no special size, but a man. Not a kid. Not Quentin. Nobody Homer knew.

Homer looked to his left down the line of searchers. He thought one of them had somehow gotten off his point when they had started again after finding Johnson's belt. No. There was Makepeace. There was Valentine's bare-kneed ringer to Makepeace's left, working his way up the hill with the others. He was where he belonged. So were the rest of them, as far as Homer could see. Whoever it was wasn't with them.

Now he thought the figure across the opening was looking toward him, but he didn't offer to come over to where Homer was. Wait. Was he carrying something? Yes, in his right hand or under his arm he carried something long like a gun or a stick. Was he a hunter? It's not the season for hunting anything.

Who are you? As he moved in and out of the shadows across the open land, the hunter, or whatever he was, seemed to grow bigger, then smaller. He'd be tall, then he'd be tiny, then tall again. Some trick of the distance, of the light. You'll see something like it with deer if you watch them in the woods: they change their size, or seem to.

He looked across at Homer, then raised his arm. He waved. Was he somebody else lost on Round Mountain? Couldn't be. Besides, if he were, wouldn't he come over? If he had been lost, well, now he was found, wasn't he? He'd be found, now. Wouldn't he be glad? He'd come on over, shake hands, express his relief, his gratitude. He didn't. He expressed nothing. He stayed over on the other side of the bright clearing. He wasn't on the search party, he was no hunter, he wasn't from town at all. He was nobody Homer knew. And yet he waved.

I don't know you. Do you know me?

Homer raised his hand and waved back to the man across the powerline.

"Hey," he called out to Makepeace. "Hey. Come over here a minute."

•••••

"You know?" Angela said. "I'm thinking. I'm thinking now: what if they don't find him? What will I do then? What will we do then?"

"That won't help," Caroline said. "You'd do better to think what you'll do if they do find him. When they do. They might have found him already."

"No," Angela said. "That's not right, see? Like, I know what we'll do if they do find him. We'll get him cleaned up, into clean clothes, dry clothes, get him to bed, get him to the doctor, get him checked out. Then, I don't know, go on like we were, I guess. But if they don't find him, that's different."

"Yes," Caroline said.

"And I know what you're thinking, too," Angela said.

"You do, huh?" Caroline said.

"Yes," Angela said. "You're thinking it just now occurred to me I don't want him found. How much easier it would be if they don't find him."

"I wish I knew what I was thinking as well as you do," Caroline said.

"Yes, and you know what?" Angela went on. "I don't mind that, either. It's like I said before. We're past that, too. Homer and me."

"You and him, huh?" said Caroline. "When did you and him start getting along so good?"

"We didn't," Angela said. "But we have left it behind too, what you are thinking, long ago. And anyway, you're wrong. I do want him back. I do want him found. I do, if it can be."

"Sure, you do, Honey," Caroline said. "You do, and you don't, just like the rest of us."

Angela looked around her, around the kitchen.

"I'm going to lie down for an hour," she said. "Wake me."

"Good," Caroline said. "Go ahead. Get some sleep. I'll wake you. It might be, you know, they've found him already. Or it might be they're finding him right now, this minute."

"Wake me," Angela said.

She left the kitchen. Caroline sat at the table alone. She put her elbow on the table and rested her chin in her hand. On the table were bread crumbs. Caroline moved them into a line with the forefinger of her other hand, then she scattered them, then moved them into a line again. She waited in the kitchen, doing that. It was eleven o'clock in the morning.

•••••

Makepeace didn't at first hear Homer call to him. He thought he had another half-hour for legs, less. Then he was going to have to take time as he. And, of course, some were, maybe most. That broken country, steep and wooded, is hard going. You don't go up those hills like you were sitting in a trolley car. It was a tough tug, as they used to say. If you weren't young and didn't do it every day, it broke you down.

Think of Johnson getting all the way up there in the state he'd reached. He never ought to have made it. He was like a ghost, like somebody had turned the flame that kept him going down so low it barely stayed lit.

Whatever was the matter with him, he wouldn't say. Probably cancer. Johnson didn't say and you didn't ask. A difficult man. Owner of large lands and farms, one of the biggest private holdings in this end of the state, some said. Employer, at one time or another, of two thirds of the men in the township. A bachelor, a rough man, limited and arrogant; limited by his arrogance and arrogant because of his limitations. And with all that, defective, so that when his illness claimed him his pride was discovered to amount to loneliness and his ownership to inability. Like a king in Shakespeare.

Of course they had never found him. When Johnson had had enough of sickness and being taken care of he'd come up here and hidden out somewhere and shot himself—or maybe he had only waited, lying on the ground. He knew where to go so they wouldn't find him. He knew Round Mountain better than any of them did; he owned it, didn't he? He had come up here to die in the right place, like one of those grand and obsolete species, the elephant, the mastodon, that take up so much space in life it seems no more than fit that, their lives at an end, they should simply disappear.

Or was it this way: that belt never was Johnson's but belonged to some randy farmboy who on coming up here to dally with the milk-maid became so heated that he lost his pants. The poor kid. The poor kid.

What?

"Look," Homer was calling to him. "Look. Can you see him?"

Makepeace left his point and joined Homer at the edge of the woods along the powerline.

"Who?" Makepeace asked. "See who?"

"He's gone," Homer said. "There was somebody over there."

"What if there was? Somebody else looking."

"No," Homer said. "He wasn't looking. Somebody else."

"Johnson?" Makepeace said.

"What?" Homer asked him. "What are you talking about?"

"Nothing," Makepeace said. "I was thinking about Johnson. When you called out, for a second, I thought you'd seen Johnson."

Homer looked briefly at Makepeace and shook his head.

"Not him, either," he said.

•••••

Valentine led them over a steep pitch where ledge showed here and there along the line and all of them were hanging on with their hands, climbing more than walking. When everyone was over, he let them rest. Not for long. Valentine saw that most were reaching the point where you couldn't let them rest too long or when the rest was done you'd never get them up again. Five minutes.

Ahead, a level stretch, then another rise, more woods: green, green, green. Going up a big hill in the woods was like some kind of trick, like an illusion, where you always think the rise ahead is the last one, the top, and it never is, there is always another rise, more woods.

Still, they were getting there now. You could tell because now, ahead of them, the daylight coming through the trees at the top was blue. That would be it, then, or not far off.

Valentine was glad of it. He was ready to get done. He had about had the course, he could feel it in his legs. They were none of them kids any more. Well, the Scouts were, the inn girls were. But not the rest of them, and not him. So if that boy was going to get found, he'd best look to it.

Valentine got to his feet.

•••••

Buster

Well, we found you, after all, didn't we?

No. I found you.

Homer saw the other fellow was back again, just out of the woods across the powerline. He motioned with his arm for Homer to leave the search and come on over there. Homer knew him now. It was Quentin, all right, but not Quentin exactly, or not only Quentin. It was also Buster. Every kid with a funny name, a fancy name, has got to have a nickname, a stout name like the other kids' names—except Quentin, who wasn't like the other kids. He wasn't like the other kids, but if he had been, they would have called him Buster.

So Homer left the line. Makepeace, puffing along, never saw him go. Neither did Valentine, neither did the others. Still, he left the search and went out into the powerline cutting, he crossed the opening to Buster, where he beckoned.

Out in the open you could see they weren't far off the top of the hill, on Homer's left as he crossed the cutting and maybe another fifty yards ahead. In the woods they were closer than they knew.

Homer came up to Buster. Buster was about what he'd expected. He was about what Quentin would have been if he'd been something other than what he was. Darker, shorter. And quiet. He still doesn't have a lot to say.

Come on, was all Buster said.

"What have you got there?" Homer asked him. And Buster showed him what he carried, not a rifle at all, but a long brass telescope.

"What's that for?" Homer asked him.

Come on, Buster said, and he started for the top of the hill. Homer followed him. He found it hard to keep up. He was a little beat, himself, from the long climb up here, and then, Buster had some years on him. Thirty-three of them, he had. A younger man by thirty-three years.

"Where are we going?" Homer asked Buster.

You'll see.

He led the way through a thick growth of tough weeds and seedling trees that lay hot and dry in the sun and filled the daylight with dust as the two of them broke through. At the top he waited for Homer. When Homer came up beside him, Buster nodded and pointed out ahead.

Homer looked.

Nearly at their feet, Round Mountain fell off like a wall, and before them, stretching away into the farthest distance, lay an entire continent extending to invisibility. Not invisibility, though, but its opposite: clarity. Homer could see, he could see it all: silver rivers, lakes, plains and easy hills spread before his gaze under the soft blue sky relieved here and there by passing clouds. Homer leaned his shoulder against a tree that grew near the edge of the precipice and looked again. You could see the country all together, the way you'd see it from an aircraft, but you could see more. Homer made out farms and villages, towns, tall cities on every side, and he could see highways lying between the cities, connecting them, vehicles going up and down the highways, and railroads, and boats on the lakes and rivers, and over the countryside the changing ways: planting and fallow, forest and grassland and waste ground. The whole country began at his feet and extended out before him for a thousand miles, two thousand miles, three—all the way to the end.

What do you think?

"What's after that?" Homer asked Buster.

Water.

Buster opened the telescope he carried to its full length and put it to his eye. He looked out over the land. He lowered the instrument and offered it to Homer. Homer shook his head.

"I don't need it," he said.

What do you think?

"It's not what I thought," said Homer. "I never knew. All this time we have been living at the end."

It looks that way.

He was a serious kid, it seemed. Not much humor to him, not a lot to say. Well, at least he was talking. They had found him, and he was safe, and he was talking now.

"Are you going down there?" Homer asked Buster.

That's right. You?

"No," Homer said. "Not me. Not now. You go ahead."

Well, then, Buster said. He closed up his glass and grinned at Homer.

I'll see you.

"Oh, yes," said Homer. "You will."

It was then Homer heard, and not only Homer, but Makepeace heard, and Valentine and the two ringers (who didn't know what it was), and the Boy Scouts and the rest of the party in the woods heard, Caroline and Angela back at the house (it woke Angela up) heard, every bird and beast wild and tame, every tree, every woodland flower on Round Mountain heard, even Johnson's belt heard (if deadmen's belts can hear), faint and far off but increasing in volume, rising in volume, now mournful and clear, the siren on the firehouse down in the village, down in the valley below.

The Deer at the End of the Day

Back of the house, their dog, Clay, Junior, an old retriever, was barking. He'd been barking for half an hour. He'd been barking the questioning, broken-record bark that meant something had come along that he didn't know what to do with. He wasn't alone in that.

Junior had been barking for half an hour, but Monica waited until Clay, her husband, was asleep again before she went to see what was on the dog's mind. She stepped out the back door into the contradictory morning: warm sun, you could almost say hot, shadeless, but from the hills the cold wet air comes down off the old snow which fills the woods, and the mud and grass are three-quarters frozen still. They were having March in April, that year.

Monica saw the dog. He was up the hill at the end of the yard, almost in the woods. He sat on his haunches and barked. Clay, Junior, the dog, sat and barked, and Clay, Senior, the man, lay in the house and slept the merciful sleep. Clay had given the dog his own name. Why shouldn't he? It was his dog.

Monica came to where the dog sat. He was at the edge of the woods, barking at a mat of juniper that the melting snow had uncovered. Monica didn't see what he had in there. Then she did. Under the low juniper branches, lying half on the snow, half off, was a deer. Not a large deer, not much larger than Clay, Junior, himself. The deer hadn't run from Junior. It didn't run from Monica. It couldn't. It had no rear legs.

Junior had stopped barking. Monica knelt beside him and looked in under the juniper at the deer. It was quite alive. Its sides rose and fell with its breathing. It didn't seem to be in pain. But its hindquarters were like a ragged gown, dragging. One leg had been torn off at the hip, and the other above the—what do you call it on a deer, the knee? The white bone protruded. There was no blood that Monica could see. All the blood had been let out of the poor thing and still it lived. It raised its head and looked at Monica with its mild black eye, then looked away, like somebody's shy child.

This is the worst thing I have ever seen, said Monica. This is the worst thing. How did it get here? What should I do? She knew the answer. She knew what she would do. She knew the next half-hour, knew it instantly, in detail, and for certain: what she would do, what Clay would say, what would happen then. She knew what Clay would say, when it was over. He'd say, "Well, as long as Homer's here..."

Clay was awake when she returned to the house—well, not awake, but not asleep. He had been made comfortable. He was floating. He was on his floating pills. The old poppy. Your modern drugs are all very well, no doubt, Clay said, but at the end of the day...

"Where were you?" Clay asked Monica. She told him.

"A deer?" Clay said. "What deer?" Monica told him again.

"I heard Junior," Clay said. "I heard him barking. I was having a dream about it."

"What shall we do?" Monica asked.

"Call Homer," said Clay.

Morphine. You can have all your up-do-date drugs, is what Clay said; they're all very well, but at the end of the day, when you have been made comfortable, when it's time to float, when floating is in order, when, indeed, not floating is unthinkable—then make it morphine. At the end of the day, the old stuff is the good stuff.

Downstairs, Monica waited at the window. Homer wouldn't be long in coming. Would he want to see Clay? Would Clay want to see him? Would the two of them want to visit, would they want to talk, even now, especially now? Would they want to joke together, even now? Monica thought not. They wouldn't talk. They wouldn't meet. They didn't have to. She knew exactly what Clay would say. She knew the words. She saw Homer's truck turn into their driveway and stop. She watched Homer get out of the truck. He was empty handed. She went to the kitchen door.

"Come in," Monica said.

"I'm muddy," said Homer. He waited on the step.

"Oh, Homer, for God's sake," said Monica. Homer came into the kitchen.

"How's Clay?" he asked Monica.

"Not terribly good."

They stood in the kitchen. Homer looked around.

"Where is he?" Homer asked.

"Upstairs," said Monica. "He's in bed."

"No," said Homer. "I mean the deer."

Monica led Homer through the kitchen, out the back door and over the yard toward the hill and the woods where the deer lay. They shut Clay, Junior, in the house.

"It might have died by now," Monica said.

"They're tough to kill, sometimes," Homer said.

They stood together at the juniper and looked down at the deer. It was still alive. It raised its head to look at them, and when it saw Homer it tried weakly to get its forelegs under it, but it couldn't. It lay back down on the snow.

"Do dogs do this?" Monica asked him.

"Sure," said Homer. "Dogs, coyotes, foxes—things of that nature. Dogs, mostly, I guess."

"Not Junior, though" said Monica. "Not Junior, I hope."

"He might," said Homer. "Any dog will run a deer in the snow.

The deer can't get over the snow. Can't get through it. They can't get away. Any dog will run a deer then. Any dog will kill one, if he can catch it."

"Not Junior," said Monica.

"Any dog at all, it looks like," said Homer. "Even the little ones, the—I don't know: what's a little kind of dog?"

"A Chihuahua. A Pomeranian."

"I wouldn't know," said Homer. "But any dog I ever heard of will run a deer, this time of the year. If he can."

"The poor little thing," said Monica. "It can't be much more than a fawn."

"Last year's buck," said Homer. "He'd have a spike in the fall."

"Clay said to call you," said Monica. "He said you'd take care of it. You're the constable, he said."

"I haven't been the constable for ten years," said Homer.

"He forgot, I guess," said Monica. "He doesn't always remember right anymore."

"Got him pretty well doped up, have they?" Homer asked her.

"All the time."

Homer nodded.

"What are you going to do with it?" Monica asked.

"Shoot it."

Monica looked him up and down. She raised her eyebrows.

"In the truck," said Homer.

Monica and Homer left the deer and walked back down toward the house. Coming off the little hill, Monica slipped, and Homer took her elbow for a moment to steady her.

"He don't feel a lot of pain, you know," Homer said when he let her go.

"He's had his legs torn off," Monica said. "How can he not feel pain?"

"No," said Homer. "I mean Clay."

•••••

At the house he didn't come in with her. He went around the side to his truck. Monica went upstairs. Clay was asleep again. She stood at the window beside the bed. It looked down on the driveway. She saw Homer beside his truck. He opened a kind of locker behind the cab and took out a big black revolver on a leather belt and a yellow box the size of the box wooden kitchen matches come in. These he took to the rear of the truck and laid them out on the down tailgate. He took two cartridges out of the box and loaded them into the revolver. Then he put the revolver back onto the belt and, carrying the belt in his hand rather than wearing it, he started back around the house toward the woods.

He didn't want me to see the gun, Monica said. He thought the gun would frighten me. He has never known what to make of me. He's Clay's friend, not mine. He doesn't even like me very much. Or is it that he does? Or is it I who don't like him? Or is it I who do? He's in charge now. He's always in charge. Of the dog, of the deer, of me, of the house. Why not? It's his house, his dog. It's his deer, it is now. Whose? Clay's? No, I mean Homer. They are the same. I know exactly what he'll say. Who? Homer? No, I mean Clay. But I know what Homer will say, too. Homer won't say anything.

Monica stood in the window. She looked at her watch: not yet ten. The mornings since Clay had become really sick were long, long; but the afternoons were longer. Annie, their Hospice worker, would arrive at ten-thirty, and then Monica would be able to get out of the house. She would have until two.

Clay slept. She couldn't see Homer. He was walking over the muddy ground, over the old, gray snow, to where the deer lay under its bush. When he got to it, he wouldn't wait. Monica imagined a noise like the bursting of a paper sack or the popping of a champagne cork, but louder.

She had met Clay when she'd gotten lost and driven off the road looking for her stepmother's place. She had wound up at the garage in the village. Clay was there. He'd driven her on to Alison's. Then later—not too much later—she'd come back to be with him. Clay was twelve years older than she. Twelve years had seemed like a lot to Monica, then they hadn't, now they did again. She jumped.

"What was that?" Clay asked from the bed.

"That was Homer shooting the poor deer," Monica said. "I told you."

"The deer," said Clay. He smiled.

She knew the words. Here they came.

"You know," said Clay, "as long as Homer was here, you ought to have asked him to take a minute more and shoot me, too, while he was at it."

"Oh, baby," Monica said, "will you for God's sake shut up?"

Clay grinned. He winked at her.

"Yeah, well," he said, "but, knowing Homer, he probably only brought the one shell. Homer's an economizing man."

Monica looked down at him. She shook her head. She kept on shaking her head until Clay turned on the pillow and looked away from her.

"Homer's a minimalist," Clay said. "Homer figures less is more."

"I don't know if I can do this," said Monica.

Clay turned his head back to her. He fixed her with his eyes. He was looking at her, now. His hair was mostly gone, and his skin was the color of the old snow that lingered in the woods, the snow the deer had lain on.

"Sure, you can," Clay said.

ABOUT THE AUTHOR

Castle Freeman, Jr. is the author of four novels (including the acclaimed *Go With Me*), a collection of essays, a major history of 250 years in a Vermont township, two story collections, and several score uncollected stories, essays, and other work set in rural northern New England. His writings have been published in periodicals including many literary magazines, *The Old Farmer's Almanac, Yankee Magazine, Vermont Life Magazine,* and *The Atlantic Monthly.* He lives in Newfane, Vermont with his wife, Alice.

Pinckney Benedict (introduction) is a renowned short-story author (*Town Smokes, The Wrecking Yard, The Miracle Boy*) and novelist (*Dogs of God*) whose work often reflects his Appalachian background. He grew up on his family's dairy farm in Greenbrier County, West Virginia. He is a professor in the English Department at Southern Illinois University, where he lives with his wife, the novelist Laura Benedict, and their family.

ACKNOWLEDGEMENTS

Eleven of the stories collected were published previously, in some cases with different titles and in slightly different forms, as follows:

"Driving Around" (*New England Review*, (Fall 2005)

"The Gift of Loneliness" (*Southwest Review*, Spring/Summer 2003)

"The Poor Brothers" (*Ontario Review*, Spring 1993)

"The Women at Holiday's" (*Ontario Review*, Spring 1997)

"The Montreal Express" (*Yankee Magazine*, March 1996)

"Bandit Poker" (*Southwest Review*, Winter 1997)

"Say Something" (*Massachusetts Review*, Autumn 1998)

"The Sister's Tale" (*The American Voice*, Spring 1999)

"Charity Suffers Long" (*Massachusetts Review*, Summer 1995)

"Round Mountain" (*American Short Fiction*, Spring 1998)

"The Deer at the End of the Day" (*Ontario Review*, Spring 2003)

Concord Free Press

The Concord Free Press is an experiment in publishing and community.

And now you're part of it.

This book is free. All we ask is that make a donation to a Hurricane Irene relief organization, such as:

Vermont Disaster Relief Fund: www.Vermont211.org

Vermont Irene Flood Relief Fund: www.vtirenefund.org

Vermont Community Foundation: www.vermontcf.org

Or another similar charity of your choosing.

When you're done, pass this book on to someone else (for free, of course), so the reading and giving goes on. It adds up.

The Concord Free Press is about inspiring generosity. Thanks for yours.

Round Mountain is a special project of the Concord Free Press, Kodak, and Vermont author Castle Freeman, Jr. For more information—and to tell us where you gave—go to:

www.concordfreepress.com/roundmountain

Where eBooks Support Free Books

The **Concord Free Press** is a labor of love supported by the generosity of hundreds of individuals. Via the Concord ePress, our ebook imprint, we sell great ebooks in collaboration with a wide range of authors—who believe in what we're doing and want to be part of it. When you buy one of our ebooks, half of the proceeds go directly to the author and the other half goes to support the **Concord Free Press**.

So check out our latest books today—and support the Concord Free Press.

www.concordepress.com

Please sign your copy of *Round Mountain* before you pass it on.

1. __________

2. __________

3. __________

4. __________

5. __________

6. __________

7. __________

8. __________

9. __________

10. __________